ANTHONY D'.

KILLING TIME

A DETECTIVE NOVEL

outskirts
press

Killing Time
A Detective Novel
All Rights Reserved.
Copyright © 2025 Anthony D'augustine
v4.0

This is a work of fiction. Names, characters, businesses, places, events, locales, and incidents are either the products of the author's imagination or used in a fictitious manner. Any resemblance to actual persons, living or dead, or actual events is purely coincidental.

The opinions expressed in this manuscript are solely the opinions of the author and do not represent the opinions or thoughts of the publisher. The author has represented and warranted full ownership and/or legal right to publish all the materials in this book.

This book may not be reproduced, transmitted, or stored in whole or in part by any means, including graphic, electronic, or mechanical without the express written consent of the publisher except in the case of brief quotations embodied in critical articles and reviews.

Outskirts Press, Inc.
http://www.outskirtspress.com

ISBN: 978-1-9772-7849-4

Cover Photo © 2025 www.gettyimages.com. All rights reserved - used with permission.

Outskirts Press and the "OP" logo are trademarks belonging to Outskirts Press, Inc.

PRINTED IN THE UNITED STATES OF AMERICA

*Dedicated to
the men and women
in law enforcement
and the military fighting
the good fight*

"And because the condition of man . . . is a condition of war of every one against every one, . . . (t)he first branch of which rule containeth the first and fundamental law of nature, which is: to seek peace and follow it. The second, the sum of the right of nature, which is: by all means we can to defend ourselves."

— Thomas Hobbes, <u>Leviathan</u> —

1

JUNE 21, 1983

11:39 AM
NEWARK, NEW JERSEY

"7-0-2 respond to 834, 6th Street. Report of a ten-three-four, unknown weapon, female victim."

"7-0-2 received."

Patrolman Mac Taylor activated the overhead lights as Patrolman Marty Presler keyed the microphone, "Any description of the perp?"

"Stand-by two."

After several seconds, the headquarters' dispatcher came back on the air. "7-0-5 back up 7-0-2."

"Five received."

"Both cars standby to copy. The perp is reported to be a white male, approximately 20 to 25 years old, last seen wearing blue jeans, white sneakers, and a black hooded sweatshirt. No further description at this time. Suspect last seen walking south on Sixth Street."

"Two to HQ, we're on Sixth now, and we have an eyeball on the suspect. Five could you respond to the scene? We'll grab this guy."

"Five received."

Patrol unit 705 arrived at 834 6th Street. A woman standing by the front door of the apartment building pointed up the stairs and said in a shaky voice, "Apartment Two-O-Six. Now! Hurry!"

Officers Mike Napoli and Pete Murphy took the stairs two at a time. The door to Apartment 206 was wide open. Both officers drew their weapons and entered the apartment. The living room was in disarray, couch and chairs overturned, lamps on the floor, a high chair lying across the entryway to the interior hall of the apartment with baby food strewn about. The officers heard loud moaning coming from a room down the hall. They both worked their way along the interior hallway to the bedroom. Napoli took the lead. Just then, Murphy heard mumbling coming from inside the hall closet. He noticed a telephone cord wrapped around the door knob of the closet with one end tied to a large display cabinet. Murphy took out his knife, cut the cord, and opened the closet door. Inside was a baby girl, no more than a year old. He quickly picked up the child.

Napoli entered the bedroom, his handgun held shoulder high. He looked down the barrel of his gun, scanning the room for any threat. Finding none, Napoli realized where the moaning was coming from. Lying on the floor in the room alongside the bed was a naked woman, her hands behind her back wrapped in white surgical tape. Her hands were bright red from the blood circulation being cut off from her bound wrists. Her head was wrapped in the same tape, only her mouth and nose exposed.

Patrolman Napoli re-holstered his weapon, took the knife from his gun belt, and cut the tape from the woman's hands. He then covered her with a bed sheet and yelled to Murphy, "Clear, clear! Victim still alive!" Murphy had already called down to the woman to come up and take the child from him. While Napoli was dealing with the victim, Murphy checked the other rooms in the apartment. Once cleared, he joined Napoli and the victim.

Keying his portable radio, he said, "Five to HQ, we need an ambulance here, pronto. Also, have a detective respond to the scene, and notify the county prosecutor's office. It looks like we have an aggravated sexual assault. Also, call child welfare. We have an infant with us."

After a few minutes, Murphy continued, "Five to Two, we're trying to get information from the victim now. She's in shock, but was able to say 'knife'. Not sure at this time if the perp had any other weapons with him. Units proceed with caution. The female witness who directed us here saw the suspect leaving the apartment. Her description is consistent with the one HQ put out."

No response.

"Five to HQ, could you relay that information to 7-0-2?"

"They might be out of the car, Five. Stay with the victim. Any other units in the area to assist O-Two?"

"Nine received."

"Eleven received."

The suspect spotted the marked police unit, turned, and ran back up 6th Street.

"I'm getting out!" yelled Patrolman Presler.

"Hold it, Marty," Taylor said as he weaved up the block, then cut into the oncoming lane and stopped his vehicle by an alleyway where the suspect had just run down.

Presler jumped out of the car and took pursuit.

The suspect ducked behind a dumpster and pulled out a knife.

Presler slowed his pace after losing sight of the young, white male. He placed his right hand on the grip of his gun. Just then he heard Officer Murphy's voice over his portable radio attached to his hip, confirming the suspect's description, and telling his unit the perp might be armed with a knife and to proceed with caution.

Presler drew his weapon and moved forward, slowly along the wall opposite the dumpster.

"Wait up, Marty," Mac said as he jogged down the alley to catch up with him.

As Presler turned back toward Mac, the suspect ran out from behind the dumpster and charged him, knife in hand.

Mac, pistol at the ready, fired two shots, hitting the suspect in the groin and right knee. The suspect dropped the knife, then fell to the ground grabbing his groin with one hand and his injured knee with the other.

Officer Presler turned, weapon in hand. He was about to put another bullet in him, but on second thought, seeing the suspect lying before him, clutching his groin and knee, Presler decided against it. Instead, he kicked the knife out of the young man's reach, rolled him on his stomach, muscled his wrists together, and cuffed him.

"Aaagh!" yelled the suspect while his hands were torn from his injuries. "I need an ambulance! Who shot me? I'll kill that bastard!"

"Shut up," Presler said just as Mac jogged up next to him, "or *I'll* put another round in you."

Mac stepped between Presler and the perp. "I shot you," he said

"I'll get you for this, you lousy prick!"

"Name the time and the place, I'll be there. I suspect that'll be at Trenton State Prison, dirt bag. Lucky for you I had to rush those shots, otherwise, you'd be dead right now." Smirking, Mac added, "So, you should thank me for not killing you."

"We're not done," said the suspect before letting out a deep moan. Then, with the words slipping between his teeth, said, "I'll see you again,"

"Yeah, in court," Mac responded. He then keyed the mic on his portable radio. "Two to HQ, we need a rig by One-Ninety-Seven

Sixth Street. Suspect was shot. He needs medical attention."

"Any officer injured?"

"That's a negative."

Presler turned to Taylor. "Thanks, Mac."

"No problem, Marty," he replied as he picked up the knife with a handkerchief from his back pocket. "He's lucky you have a conscience, or else he'd have three bullets in him, only the third one would be in his head."

Presler brushed off the comment. Looking at the suspect, he then began reciting Miranda, "You have the right to remain silent. . . ."

Less than a minute later, backup patrol units 709 and 711 rolled up to the alleyway.

2
JULY 27, 2015

10 AM
NEW YORK, NEW YORK

The upper bay of the New York/New Jersey harbor offers a spectacular view of the Statue of Liberty, Ellis Island, Governor's Island, and the southern tip of Manhattan Island. Informally called the New York Harbor, the upper bay is situated at the confluence of the Hudson and the East Rivers. To the west lies the Kill Van Kull, which is an extension of Newark Bay. The Harbor is the gateway to extensive commercial cargo traffic to the west at Port Newark and cruise shipping lines to the north along the Westside of Manhattan. In addition, the harbor offers an abundance of sightseeing water tours, ferries, and pleasure boating.

This summer's day, the sky was crystal clear with a warm breeze. Quite a variety of private motor boats were out on the bay along with the daily commercial tour boats and ferries shuffling people from New York and New Jersey ports to work and to the historic landmarks. Moreover, with the soft breeze that skipped across the surface of the water, white sails could be seen everywhere.

Danny Brown was piloting his 36-foot motor yacht—the *Sea Witch*—by Ellis Island. His buddy, Bill Puchia, was lounging on the back deck.

"Wow! That'd make some picture!" Bill yelled up to Danny on the fly bridge.

"What's that?!" Danny yelled back, loud enough for Bill to hear him over the sound of his twin diesel engines.

"The Circle Liner passing in front of Lady Liberty! Red and white boat, dark blue water, blue sky with white puffs, and Proud Mary all dressed in green holding a gold torch! I wish I had my camera with me!"

Danny smiled as he looked across the bay. It was a beautiful site. He wished he could stay out on the water longer, but he had to start heading up to his slip by the Tappan Zee Bridge so he'd have time to clean the boat, drop Bill off, and meet his wife for dinner. Danny headed north toward the Hudson River. It was then he saw to his right what looked like a log floating in the water. He slowed his engines to wake speed as he maneuvered his boat closer to the object. Realizing the object wasn't a log, but a body floating face down, he cut the engines.

"Grab the hook!" he yelled down to Bill.

"What?! Why?!"

"Just do it!" Danny yelled as he slid down the ladder leading to the main deck.

Bill handed him the gaff hook.

"Oh man, look at this," he said to Bill.

The corpse bobbed with the movement of the waves.

Danny then pulled the body close to the boat.

"Hold this," he said to Bill as he handed him the hook with the body in tow. "I have to head back up top and radio in what we found. The NYPD Harbor Police needs to be called."

A 27-foot Harbor Police boat happened to be cruising around the Statue of Liberty when it got the call to respond. The Aviation and SCUBA teams were also notified and told to respond to the scene. Within the next five minutes, the patrol boat pulled within twenty feet of the *Sea Witch*.

Other boats in the area had heard the call over the radio and started to head in the direction of the *Sea Witch*, either to help or to gawk.

Harbor Police boat captain Sergeant Rich Halley got on the loudspeaker. "All boats in the immediate area, except for the *Sea Witch*, please move away from the area!"

The surrounding boats edged away from the scene, but still stayed in the area.

Sergeant Halley noticed Puchia was trying to keep the body from sliding under the swim platform. "Be careful not to pull too hard on that body. We'll have someone here soon to take it out of the water."

Then, out of earshot from the *Sea Witch*, Halley turned to NYPD Officer Eldridge standing on the deck and said, "Ken, make sure you get those guys' names and addresses for the Bureau."

Within several more minutes, an NYPD helicopter was overhead and two SCUBA officers descended into the water. Photographs were taken, latitudes and longitudes documented, and the body was removed from the water and placed on the patrol boat.

Though the deceased exhibited extreme skin slippage and had expanded twice its size, due to gases that built up within the body during decomposition, the officers were able to determine that the victim was a woman. Her right foot was missing, and she had torn flesh throughout her body, the result of crabs and fish feeding off the corpse. During their preliminary examination of the body, the patrol officers observed what appeared to be an entry wound in the back of the woman's head and a much larger exit wound just above her left eye.

NYPD Officer Ken Eldridge then disembarked the Harbor Police boat and boarded the *Sea Witch*. For the next half-hour he took down all the particulars of the discovery from Brown and Puchia.

Shortly after that, he returned to the Harbor Police boat and radioed to headquarters to have the NYPD Homicide Squad notified of the death and initial determination of cause—a gunshot wound to the back of the head. The body was then transported to the NYC Chief Medical Examiner's Office.

Not long after the helicopter, SCUBA team, 36-foot yacht, and 27-foot Harbor Police boat left the waterway, the wind began to pick up and so too the height of the waves. Unlike other areas where visible signs of a crime still remained, none were left on the surface of the water.

The body was later identified as Shawna Braxton, from McKinley Avenue, Newark.

3
AUGUST 1, 2015

6:16 AM
NEWARK/VERONA, NEW JERSEY

The phone rang six times.

"Are you up?"

"What in God's name do you want? Do you know what time it is? I told you I don't want to deal with you anymore. I don't want to be involved in this," said Alan Springer.

"I need you to do some more look ups for me," said Alex Brisco.

"Now?! Come on, Mr. Brisco. Haven't I done enough for you?"

"I'll tell you when you've done enough. Don't give me any shit, or I'll pay you a visit. I don't want to do that. But I will. And don't think about ratting me out to the police. I have friends in dark places who like nothing better to do than squaring up with rats."

"Okay, but this is it. I could go to jail for what you're asking me to do."

"Jail ain't so bad. Stiffing me would be a lot worse. But, okay, I'll make this my last request." He lied.

"What do you need this time?" asked Springer.

"I need to know where I can find Martin Presler."

"I gave you that information the last time you asked. His records show that he's been in Sarasota, Florida."

"I know that, but I need locations he might be at besides his home address."

"I told you where he buys his food; what department stores he shops at; the movie theater he goes to; where he gets his oil changed. What more do you need?"

"I want to know where he hangs out. Where he might go to relax."

"All right, hang on. Let me get on the computer."

After a few minutes, Springer said, "His profile says he likes hiking, trips to the beach, fishing, and swimming. I suspect he'll be hiking nature trails, fishing in lakes and ponds, or swimming at the beach. He might even enjoy some surf casting at the beach."

"What beach do you think he'd prefer to go to, if that's the case?"

"Wait a minute. Let me check his spending records. That's the best way to zero in on his locations and what he likes. Now, looking at his recent bills, I see he's accumulated a lot of credit-card charges in downtown Venice. Also, charges at a golf course and restaurant right by the Venice Municipal Airport. I'm looking at a map of that area right now. There's a beach just south of the airport. Looks like a good place to fish. Name search says it's the Shark Tooth Capital of the World. What's that all about? It says people like to sift for sharks' teeth there. How weird is that?"

"What's the name of the beach? What's it called?" asked Brisco.

"Caspersen Beach." Springer enlarged the map he was looking at. "It looks quite nice for a quiet getaway."

"That's it. That's what I'm looking for — quiet and secluded," said Brisco.

10:11 AM
Matanza, Cuba

In the year 2000, the United Nations passed the Victims of Trafficking and Violence Protection Act that set international standards for nations to report and eliminate those practices of abuse. It's a three-tiered system. Tier One lists the nations that comply with the Act. Tier Two lists those that partially comply with the standards. Tier Three nations neither comply with the recommended standards nor make any effort to do so. Cuba is a Tier Three nation. One of the main routes for trafficking Cuban citizens into the U.S. is through Mexico, through the Mexican cartels. Cubans are shipped or flown to Mexico, then smuggled across the U.S. border, into either Texas, New Mexico, or Arizona.

There is a second system, however, in which Cubans are trafficked directly into the United States. This system is comprised of independent boat captains who pilot what are called, "ir barcos rápidos" — "go-fast boats." Hector Jiminez is one such boat captain.

"How many do you have lined up to go, Lucia?"

"Three right now, but there are others interested in making the trip. They have to check with relatives for the money."

"Well, see how many more you can line up by the twelfth."

"Why that late in the month?" she asked.

"It'll give you time to get more bodies, which means more money, and it'll give me time to connect with the powers that be. Besides, no full moon then. Not for another two weeks after. It'd be a good, dark night to travel."

4

AUGUST 4, 2015

10:30 AM
CASPERSEN BEACH IN VENICE, FLORIDA

It was a typical August, Florida beach day: hot, sunny, and blue skies filled with swooping pelicans and cormorants. Along the beach in shallow waters were several people sifting sand, looking for sharks' teeth. There were others on shore running their fingers through the rocks, shells, and bones that they dug up hoping to find an elusive black tooth. At the north end of the beach sat Martin Presler. Ensconced in a short-legged beach chair, Presler cast his fishing line into the water for the tenth time and sat back. *This is the life*, he mused.

    Brisco, wearing swim trunks, a sleeveless undershirt, and an unbuttoned Hawaiian shirt looked out onto the Gulf from the raised walkway behind the beach. He carried a dark blue towel over his right arm and hand. Limping down the stairs onto the hot sand, he headed toward Presler. Nearing some fifty yards of his target, he squeezed hard on the sharp, hunter's knife hidden under the blue towel. Just then, a family carrying beach chairs, blankets, and a beach umbrella appeared from another set of entry stairs to his immediate right.

"Good morning," said a member of the family as they approached him.

Brisco nodded and walked by.

Hearing the salutation which carried across the opened area, Presler turned his head. That's when he saw Brisco limping toward him.

As the man got closer, Presler said, "Hi."

Brisco turned his head away from him and just nodded.

Looking behind the limping individual, Presler called out to the approaching family, "I wondered when you guys were going to get here, Dee!"

The tall brunette replied, "Remember what it was like getting me and Katie ready for the beach, Dad? Try getting *three* girls ready . . . and carrying all this extra beach paraphernalia."

As Presler and his daughter Denise were exchanging words, Brisco had an immediate choice to make: kill or move on. Timing is everything. In that moment, he reconsidered his plan to walk unnoticed behind Presler, catching him off guard, at which point he planned to reach around him, stab him in the heart, and then slice his throat. The element of surprise, however, was dampened considerably. Presler was now looking at him, a fish knife and needle-nosed plyers within his reach. Moreover, Presler's daughter, son-in-law, and their three daughters were behind him. He had noticed the strapping young man of the family group had been carrying a beach umbrella, the lower section of which was a pointed metal tube about three feet long; a potential weapon, more dangerous than his six-inch, bladed hunter's knife.

Brisco hadn't any concerns about killing three innocent adults and three children. He actually relished the idea of taking out Presler, his daughter, and her family, but he wasn't sure he could eliminate all six, or at least a few of them, with his knife, survive the attack at all, or get away unscathed before eyewitnesses began to pile up. He knew the spree would attract way more attention than one quick attack on a guy sitting in a beach chair. Reluctantly, he turned and headed to the stairs that brought the family to the beach.

Marty Presler kept his eyes on him as he limped up the stairs. There was something about him that didn't seem quite right to the former detective lieutenant. Whatever it was that bothered Presler, he just couldn't put his finger on it.

"Catch anything?"

Presler turned back. "What?"

"Catch anything, Dad?"

Marty looked up at his daughter and laughed. "No, no luck, so far, honey."

"Maybe *we'll* bring you some luck," she said. Denise and her family then began to set up the beach umbrella and chairs, and lay down blankets,

Brisco hobbled to his blue van parked across the rock road of Caspersen Beach. It was there he began to plan a second attempt to kill Presler . . . and to kill someone else, much farther north.

2:07 PM
Bloomfield, New Jersey

"Get down from up there," Mac Taylor said.

"I'm okay, Dad. I just wanted to see if I could make it to this branch."

"That's too high for you, Hope. If you fall, you'll break a leg. And I'm not prepared to call your mom and tell her we're at the hospital."

"Okay, I'm coming down." Hope then shimmied her way down the maple tree in the park.

Mac was glad to get the day off to spend some time with his

daughter while his wife, Cheryl, was out food shopping. The P.I. business so far this summer had been busy, so a day off with Hope was appreciated. He hadn't had much time to spend with her. He did not want to make the same mistake he did with his first daughter. Too much work, too little time with family caused Rachel to get involved with a very bad element. Mac had taken care of that group of miscreants, but too late to save his pregnant daughter. Right now, he had cleared up all his open cases and was looking forward to at least a week or two off for vacation with Cheryl and Hope.

"Let's go grab lunch," Mac said as Hope brushed the debris from her hands, shirt, and shorts.

They headed to the local café located several blocks from their house. It was a quant, little café that, in addition to breakfasts, offered various sandwiches for lunch. The shop usually closed around three o'clock, unless it was a busy day at which time the doors stayed open until four. It was not busy this day, though. The waitress was cleaning off the tables and hoping for an early closing when Mac and Hope walked in. After heading to the bathrooms to wash up, they took seats by the front door.

"How's it going, Lauren?" Mac asked the waitress.

"Not bad. It was busy earlier today. Been quiet the last half-hour. What can I get you two?"

They ordered two sandwiches, fries, pickles, and bottled soda.

Mac then asked Hope, "Are you ready for school this year? New classroom, new teacher."

"Yes, Dad. And Mom will be working there in the nurse's office. I don't know how I feel about that."

"What do you mean?"

"Well, you know I love her, but I don't know how it'll be, seeing her all day, every day in school."

"It'll be fine. She won't bother you."

"Will you tell her that?"

"Yes, sure. I'll let her know you're a big girl now and she need not hover over you. Okay?"

"Thanks, Dad."

5
AUGUST 5, 2015

3:17 PM
HAVANA, CUBA

Marietta Consuelo Alvarez was born in Havana in 1943, a time when Cuba was a friend of the United States, time when Cuba fought with the allies against the Axis powers of World War II. In 1953, Fidel Castro led a six-year revolution that saw final victory on January 1, 1959, with the overthrow of Fulgencio Bastista. On April 17, 1961, Cuban exiles of the Cuban Democratic Revolutionary Front, supported financially by the U.S. government, conducted a military landing in Cuba in an attempt to retake power from the Castro revolutionaries. The failed attempt took place in an area known as the Bay of Pigs, during which 1,100 Cubans exiles were captured during the invasion. Marietta's husband, Juan Escalante Alvarez, was one of them. He was denied visitation to his pregnant wife during his imprisonment. When Marietta gave birth to their daughter, Andrianna, Marietta remained in Havana, but Juan was expatriated to the United States in exchange for food and supplies. All attempts to reunite with his wife and daughter failed. He died in Miami twelve years to the day he and his compatriots stormed the ill-fated Cuban beach.

In March of 1978, Andrianna Consuelo Alvarez married Raul

Morales Rodriguez. They lived in a small apartment in one of the poorer sections of Centro Habana. It was there, in May of 1979, that their daughter Maria Consuelo Alvarez Rodriguez was born. Two years later, while holding Maria to her chest, Andrianna slipped off a broken street curb, landed on her back, and suffered a major spinal cord fracture. The injury resulted in chronic back pain and a failure to walk long distances. But what distressed Andrianna the most was that she could no longer pick up and hold her baby. Depression set in with a lifetime of painkillers and antidepressants. Her back pain and anxieties increased over the years. Then, in 1991, after ten years of depression, Andrianna's heart gave out and she died.

Maria's father, Raul, was a heavy smoker his whole life. He had been sick for many years prior to his death which was attributed to emphysema, pneumonia, and respiratory failure. Though still a young girl in her teenage years, Maria had been his caretaker until his death in 1995. After Raul passed away, Maria felt she could no longer live in her father's apartment. She needed to be among family, so she moved in with her only living relative, her father's sister Rosa. Though Maria was only sixteen years old at the time of his death, Tía Rosa was able to get her a job where she worked. It was a local textile mill. Maria spent the next five years of her life sewing pockets in jeans and dress slacks. Because of the quality and speed of her work, Maria was promoted to dressmaker. It was grueling work those last five years at the company, and she was offered little additional pay for the extra hours worked. Still, it was a job she truly loved.

On July 12, 2015, Tía Rosa, died; killed, actually, the result of a robbery that turned deadly. Rosa did not live long enough to fulfill her dream of seeing changes in Cuban laws that would allow her to own and operate her own dress shop. Those changes eventually came about, but too late for Tía Rosa.

Two weeks after her aunt died, Maria was threatened with

losing her job as a seamstress if she didn't up her hours for little more pay. With nothing but a few pesos to her name and rent due in two weeks, Maria decided to look for work elsewhere; for a job less demanding of her time and for more pay. On her late evenings off, she walked the streets in the downtown barrios of Havana looking for those opportunities. That's when, looking at the cracked pavement below her feet, Maria ran directly into a well-dressed young woman.

"Excuse me. I'm so sorry."

"Are you okay?" the woman asked Maria.'

"Yes, . . . well not really. Why do you ask?"

"I've been watching you. You've been up and down the street all evening. Are you looking for someone?"

"No, I'm looking for a job. Do you have one for me?"

"What do you do? What kind of work are you looking for?"

"I'm a seamstress. That's what I've been doing my whole working life. Do you know of any seamstress jobs? Or any job that I can do? I'm young. I'm able to do all kinds of manual work."

"You say you're a seamstress. Hmmm. I don't know if you'd be interested but I'm connected with the Cuban community in Miami. They are always looking for good seamstresses in their factories. And the pay is one hundred times better than here in Cuba."

"That sounds great but I'm in Cuba, not America. Thank you, anyway," Maria said as she prepared to walk on.

"Wait, wait," said the woman. "I can get you to America, if that's what you want. You might not want to go if you have a big family here. Do you?"

"Do I what?"

"Do you have a big family here?"

"No. It's just me. I don't have a problem leaving. It's just not going to happen. I hear there is now a ferry service from here to the U.S., which was just passed a few months ago, but I have no passport, no visa, no money, and no private boat or a plane willing to take me out of here."

"I might know a way to make it all happen."

"What are you talking about? Are you serious?"

"Well, for five hundred pesos or fifty American dollars, I know someone who has a boat and would be willing to take you to the Keys. I can make a call and someone will pick you up once on land and take you to U.S. Customs or to a shop in Miami where you can make some good money. I can set you up, but if and when I do, you'll have to come up with the money."

"I don't have that kind of money. Besides, who are you? I don't like talking about my money with a stranger."

"My name is Vinita Garcia Pérez. And you?"

"I'm Maria, Maria Consuelo Alvarez Rodriguez."

"How much money *do* you have, Maria Consuelo?"

"Not much, a few pesos. That's all I have left . . . and that's what's left for food and a roof over my head."

"I'll tell you what I'll do. I'll loan you the money, but once you get in the States and start getting paid, you'll pay me back with some interest. Okay?"

"That sounds too good. Why would you do that for me? You don't even know me."

"For two reasons. I have friends in the States who could use the help. And two, I get a commission for helping find workers for them. Plus, I know if I loan you the money, I'll get it back with interest."

"I'll think about it. But if I agree, and I'm not saying I will, I'm not giving you anything until I'm aboard a boat taking me to Miami."

"But, of course," said the woman. "Think about it. If you decide moving to America and making a lot of money is for you, meet me by the bus stop over there, next week, August 11th, at ten o'clock in the evening. Bring whatever money you do have. I'll bring the balance of what you need. All five hundred pesos, if necessary. You won't need those pesos in the U.S., so you just might want to get rid of them and owe less."

"I'll have to think about it, Vinita. I just might see you by that bus stop on the 11th," said Maria, "unless I find a good job here before then."

8:34 PM
Miami, Florida

"I need a girl for the Orlando club," said Benito Valverde. "I'm short on the early shift now that Georgia tried to take off. I was forced to either kill her or sell her off. No money to be made killing her, so I sold her off to a high-end broker. She's on some island now where she can't run too far. I let the other girls believe I had her killed. Good for business."

"I haven't seen any girls on the street lately," said Maggie Selina. "I really haven't been looking. I've been busy with the girls we have here . . . and the books. It's been a hectic week overall."

"How about you, Jake?" Valverde asked his muscle.

"Nothing, Boss. The streets up there in Orlando have been empty. I just got back down here yesterday after dealing with the Georgia handoff. I've been busy since then coordinating the shipment scheduled to come."

"What to do? What to do?"

"How about our Cuban connection? What's his name . . . Jiminez?"

"Yeah, yeah," said Valverde. "I'll have to give him a call. In the meantime, put the word out with our boys to keep an eye on the street for any runaways."

"Will do."

Valverde then turned to Maggie. "I've been meaning to talk to you about that shipment of drugs coming in. You need to square away the cash on that deal. Plus, I need several of our people to move the product. Jake, is that taken care of?"

"Done. I have Miguel and Samuel lined up to handle the swap and drop."

"We might need a few more people to help out around here, covering the clubs, while you guys are busy with the shipment. You know Snake. I'll give him a call. He could help, and he might have a friend or two from his prison days who might be willing to lend a hand. I'll let you know how that pans out after I call him."

"Okay. Where do you want to stash the drugs this time?"

"Temporarily at my place. I hope to have the shit moved out in short order for distribution. Once again, Snake might be the man to talk to. He's been distributing the juice I've been giving him for his gym-rat friends. I don't mind him using *that* shit. It's good for his tough-guy image. I just write it off his take. But H and coke might not work. He'd get a house fee, but I just have to make sure he's not one of those users. That could be a problem. I don't need the bulk of my profits going into his arm or up his nose. Plus, users are losers. They're thieves. They can't be trusted. All of them. They can't help themselves."

"What about the cash sales?" Maggie asked.

"Keep 'em at my house until I figure out a way to clean that money through some legit source. I can use some of it to buy more dope, but it's still growing faster than I can pay for the shit and for all my people. Add to the drug sales, the money from all the girls, and, I'm tellin' ya, I have to find a legit source. Otherwise, those bums in the IRS and FBI will trace everything I own and make it theirs. With that RICO. statute, they'll take everything. I mean *everything*! Meanwhile, I'll be sitting in the can for years for tax evasion. I'll tell ya right now, that's not going to happen! I go down, we all go down. So, make sure everybody up and down the line understands that."

"Got it, Boss," said Jake.

"Everything's going to go smoothly. Trust me," said Maggie. "Hopefully, we can replace Georgia, soon. Plus, your friend Snake will be able to help. And, you know me. I'll do whatever you need done."

"That's what I like about you, Maggie. Always optimistic. And loyal. That's why you're the one I trust with my money."

6
AUGUST 6, 2015

7:07 AM
MIAMI, FLORIDA

Jill and Maureen sloughed down on the park bench in the early morning hour. The young runaways from Model City, a rough neighborhood in the northwest section of Miami, had just about run out of the money they stole from their parents. Living the last few days on park benches and in abandoned locations throughout the city of Miami, the girls knew they needed an influx of cash to survive or they'd have to head back to Model City, to a life they no longer wished to live.

The girls grew up best friends in an area of Miami that was rife with drugs and violent crime. They weren't in the in-crowd, did not compete in sports, and they happened to be in the lower end of the GPA scale. With still two years left in high school, the girls did not see college in their future, nor did they want to spend their prime years waiting tables in some small restaurant just off the highway. They wanted more from their lives. So, they took what money was stashed around in their homes and hopped on buses heading to downtown Miami. Several days later, awakening on a park bench with only a few dollars left to their name, the two girls realized they were not going to make it.

"We need money if we're going to be able to stay here," said Jill as the two stood and stretched out.

"How much do we have left?" asked Maureen.

"Just enough for coffee and a donut."

"One donut?"

"No, no. Thankfully, enough for two."

The girls then headed to the donut shop. They stayed there until mid-morning trying to decide if they should look for work or head back north and face the music. They knew missing persons alerts might have been put out for them. Then again, they weren't even sure if their parents cared enough to make the effort. They did not want to face the wrath or, worse yet, the apathy of their parents if they were to return. They knew laughter would await them from schoolmates for their failed attempt to make it out in the world. So, they decided to look for work and hopefully a more permanent place to stay.

"Hey, girls," said the young man who just ordered a dozen assorted donuts. "Are you the two that were hanging in the park this morning?"

"How do you know that?" asked Jill.

"I know everything about this area. This is my beat."

"What, are you a cop?"

"No, no way. I work for a guy who kinda runs this section of town."

"What does he run? Is he hiring? Because we're looking for a job."

"He's got all kinds of jobs. I'm sure he'll have a job for you girls. If you're finished here follow me. I'm heading to his place of business right now."

"Great!" said Maureen as the two girls followed the young man to Benito Valverde's strip club, Amantes Latinas.

It was a quiet morning in the club. The bar and dance floor were empty. The girls were escorted to the back room where Benito and Maggie were going over the prior night's take.

"Whoa, who do we have here, Samuel?!" Valverde said, looking up from the cash on the table.

"Here's your coffee, boss," the young man said as he put the coffee and bag of donuts on the table. "I met these girls at the shop. They're looking for a job. I thought you'd be interested in hiring them."

"Where are you young ladies from?" Valverde asked.

"Model City," said Jill.

"So, you're here looking for work?"

"We need a job. We've been in the city now for several days and we kinda ran out of money. I don't know what kinda work you might have for us, but we could use some money and a place to stay right now."

Valverde picked up a handful of cash from the table. "Here, take this," he said handing the money to Jill and Maureen. "There's a lot more where that came from, if you're willing to work here."

"What do we have to do?"

"Well, first order of business, how old are you girls?"

"We're eighteen," Jill lied.

"Why do you need a place to stay? No family?"

"No, no. We left Model City and don't intend to go back . . . that is if we can earn some money and find a place to stay around here."

Valverde looked over at Maggie, then back to the girls. "Did you have breakfast?"

"Just a donut and cup of coffee each."

"Maggie, take these girls downstairs while I have Samuel go grab them some real food. You can explain to these young ladies what they'll be doing and where they'll be staying."

After Maggie and the girls left the room, Valverde turned to

Samuel. "Jake tells me you're in on the drug pickup. Before you head out on that, do a quick check around the neighborhood. Make sure nobody is looking for these chippies." Then, handing Samuel a bunch of ten-dollar bills from the table, Valverde said, "Here you go, kid. Great job! These girls should bring in some good money."

7
AUGUST 10, 2015

2:05 AM
NORTH ARLINGTON, NEW JERSEY

Flames curled along the eaves of the one-story home. Located on the tree-lined street of the suburban neighborhood, the ranch-styled house was soon fully engulfed in smoke and fire. Radiant heat from the fire melted the aluminum siding on the bi-level home located fifteen feet south of the one-story house. The local fire department personnel responded, but their best efforts were not enough to save the structure. The fire had rendered the building no longer salvageable. Once it was safe to enter the burned-down dwelling, firefighters searched for hidden pockets of fire to extinguish. It was then Firefighter Giffen removed some charred debris and found a body.

4:27 PM

"Well, I'm glad you could make it. Long time no see, Investigator Taylor."

"Detective Frank Arnet of the Bergen County Prosecutor's Office. What do I owe the pleasure of your company?" Mac replied somewhat sarcastically.

"I called you because this case might be of some concern to you."

"Just looking at this building—if you can call it that—I'm thinking fire investigation, accidental or arson, in which case the Arson Squad would be here, not Homicide. You're still in Homicide, right?"

"Yep, head of it. Detective Lieutenant."

"Congratulations. Sorry I didn't acknowledge your rank, Lieutenant. But I still don't know why either of us is here."

"First off, there was a victim. He died in the fire, but not as a result of the fire. He was dead before the fire started . . . that's why the Arson Squad turned the case over to my guys."

"What was the cause of death if not asphyxiation from smoke?'

"Well, an autopsy was done this afternoon. The cause was from asphyxiation, but not from the fire. He wasn't breathing at the time of the fire. No charring or cherry redness in his throat or lungs according to the medical examiner. And no soot around his mouth or nose."

"What are you thinking, a bag?"

"Probably a plastic bag. There are some subcutaneous ligature wounds around his wrists and ankles. He was tied up at one point."

"But not when they found him?"

"Nope. The ties were either removed or consumed in the fire. No traces at all."

"Odd how most things burn up in fire, but bodies cook like meat on a grill unless under constant, direct burning of close to two thousand degrees for four or more hours. They don't just burn up. That's what I've been told. Well, at least the skin damage on his wrists helps to prove your homicide and rule out an accidental death or suicide."

"Yeah, part one of the case is solved."

"How about lividity? Was the body intact enough to determine that?"

"We did get a break. A section of the ceiling collapsed on him and protected the body from major burning. Looks like he was killed where he was lying. The autopsy confirmed that the settled blood pooling is consistent with the position he was found in."

"All the more reason there should have been some remains of the ties. I would conclude, then, that any bindings were definitely removed before the fire was set."

"And that's why my squad got the case and not Arson."

Mac walked to where the front door had been located prior to the fire and looked into the charred remains of what once used to be a foyer and living room. Lieutenant Arnet followed closely behind.

"What about the fire?" Mac asked. "What did the Arson guys determine the cause to be?"

"Multiple areas of origin, the initial fuel sources were suspected to be curtains and bed linens, paper products throughout the house, pizza boxes on the kitchen stove with all pilots turned on. Secondary fuel sources were kitchen cabinets, furniture, and carpeting. No indications of an accelerant being used. Flashover occurred around the time the fire department arrived so it's hard to determine exact points of fire origin, but judging from the witness reports, the fire appeared to have started in several rooms at the same time." Arnet then looked down at his police-issued note pad. "To quote one of the Arson guys, 'Early reports by neighbors and first responders indicate flame vectoring was consistent throughout the structure, confirming multiple points of fire origin.' You'll have to talk with those guys for the specifics they'll be testifying to, should this case ever reach trial."

"Any suspects?" Mac asked.

"That's the reason I asked you here today. We have one. A solid one. One you may remember from an early time in your career."

"And who might that be?"

"Alex Brisco."

"Brisco, Brisco. The rapist?"

"Come on Mac. You can't be serious. How many men have you shot in your life?"

"You don't want to know. But you're right. I remember him. That does go back. He was the rapist Marty Presler and I arrested some thirty or thirty-five years ago."

"Bingo. One and the same. It took our squad until late this morning to tie him to the victim and then to you and Presler."

"You're telling me Brisco is out of prison?! After being convicted for criminal restraint, agg. assault, agg. sexual assault, weapon possession, attempted assault on a police officer . . . shall I go on? He should be rotting in jail."

"Mac, he was sentenced to thirty years, no parole; which means, with time served, he was out last year."

"Why wasn't Marty or I notified of his release?"

"Just the victim, her family, and witnesses were told about it. Sorry, retired cops don't count."

"Did you lock him up?"

"Not yet."

"Is he in your sights?"

"It's a long story."

"Just give me the short version."

"Okay, after Brisco got out of prison, he was clean for about a year, or so he made it seem. In 2014, he left the country, skipped to Mexico. It was then one of our DEA agents was killed down there and Brisco's name popped up in the investigation. Then recently, the female witness in your case back in 1983 was found floating in the New York Harbor."

"So, you're telling me all this now, why?

"I think you or your buddy Presler might be on this guy's target list."

"Because the female witness washed ashore?"

"Yeah, with a bullet wound to the back of her head. Not likely a suicide," Arnet said sarcastically.

"What proof do you have that it's Brisco who killed her? I suspect you have reason to rule out a jealous lover, disgruntled pimp, . . . an irate friend or relative."

"Yep, plus we ruled out her murder as the end result of a robbery, drug deal, or combination of the two," added Arnet. "Look, I know the physical evidence is not there . . . yet, but the motive is. She was the one who reported the attack on the rape victim, and she testified at his trial that she saw him leaving the apartment right after the rape."

"That's it? That's all you've got?"

"That, plus this victim."

"Why, who is he?"

"His name is Jonathan Tucker. Does his name ring a bell?"

"Jonathan Tucker. Isn't that the name of the victim's husband back in that rape case?"

"That's him. Remember the circumstances around that investigation?"

"Of course. We learned his wife, Sally Tucker, was raped by Brisco for payback. Brisco wouldn't talk much, but the one thing he did say was that Tucker owed him money. Tucker denied owing him money, but since it was suspected that both were involved in drug trafficking at the time, it looked like Tucker stiffed him in a deal. Brisco threatened to rape Tucker's wife if he didn't come across with the cash. Tucker never did, and Brisco made good on his threat. The sicko then threw her baby in the closet, knocked her out with one punch, taped her up, and raped her. I'm glad I put a bullet in that mutt's groin."

"That's it in a nutshell. And now we have two dead from that case. That leaves the wife, who, by the way, never recovered from the assault. She had gotten a divorce from Tucker years ago and now lives with her sister in Virginia. Ever since Brisco was released from prison, she has been living in constant fear. I think he had done enough to ruin her life. I don't suspect that she will be victim number three, but who knows. The locals down there in Virginia are keeping an eye on her, plus the Feds had been notified to help out in any way they can."

"So, you have all your bases covered."

"Now I do. I'm telling you all this because you might be a target of this lunatic. Remember you did put two slugs in him. He's still walking with a limp from one of those slugs, and I'm not sure if your second bullet ended his love life. He has more reason to be less forgiving of you than he did for these last two victims. And you do have a family to worry about. This guy has already shown that he will go after family. So, if you need me for anything, I'm here for you."

"How about Marty Presler? Has he been notified?"

"Not yet. He's retired now from what I'm told. I could track him down through your old department, but I thought you might want to reach out to him. You and I have worked together in the past. I still have your number. You and Presler were partners in your old department. I thought you might like to bring him up to snuff. Tell him to feel free to call me at any time, for anything. Just call the homicide squad."

"So Brisco was suspected of being in Mexico, now in the U.S. where bodies are popping up in Newark Bay and North Arlington. And you're telling me that Marty, my family, and I might be the next targets of this psychopath. I was hoping this bullshit would end once I retired. The fun never seems to stop, does it, lieutenant?"

4:59 PM
Bloomfield, New Jersey
and
Venice, Florida

"Marty, it's me, Mac."

"Hey bro. How have you been?"

"Did I wake you, old-timer?"

Marty laughed. "How old do you think I am? In bed at 5 o'clock? I'm not *that* old . . . yet. Actually, I'm usually in the sack around one or two AM. Man, it's good to hear from you. I haven't heard from you in quite a while. It must be something important, though, for you to call me at dinner time. You know how much I enjoy my meals. Seriously, though, are you okay? Is everything okay?"

"Been better. I was hoping to take a week or two vacation with the family, but something came up that needs our attention. Never fails. I can never leave this job. Unless I take your advice and retire, full-time. Speaking of that, how has retirement been treating you?""

"Best thing I've ever done. Don't get me wrong, I miss the job, the action, but it's nice getting up when I want, traveling, playing golf, spending time with the grandkids, fishing." Martin Presler realized, though, that this was not a social call. "Enough small talk, my brother. You called me for a reason. What's up?"

"Well, I hate to shake up your Disney world, but I just met with a detective from the Bergen County Homicide Squad. He had some disturbing information about an old defendant of ours."

"You're kiddin'? What defendant? What information?"

Mac then told Presler everything Detective Lieutenant Arnet had relayed to him.

"Hard to believe that dirtbag Brisco is now out and about." Presler said. "I wonder what he looks like today. It's been, what, about fifty years since we last saw him."

"Not quite that long, but it's been some time. He's been out for at least a year, maybe two. That's the system for you. I've been told he still walks with a limp from the bullet I put in his knee. Tell you what I'll do. I'll run some checks on him, reach out to a few contacts, and try to tap into whatever criminal enterprise this mutt is involved in. You know he's got to be dealing in something."

"Wait a second, Mac. Did you say he still walks with a limp?"

"Yeah, why?"

"Maybe this is nothing, but just the other day at the beach, some guy with a limp was walking toward me. I didn't see him until I heard my son-in-law say 'Good morning' to him. When I turned and spotted him, he quickly turned leaving the beach after passing my daughter and her family. He nodded and turned away from me when I said 'Hi.' Nothing *too* unusual about that, but you know how cop instinct works. Something just didn't seem right about him."

"I'm not liking that, Marty. Sounds like our boy. Stay put, I'll head down. Are you still carrying?"

"Yep, not all the time, though. Certainly not when I'm in my bathing suit on the beach. I will bring a beach bag with me, though, the next time with either my .40 cal or 9mm in it. The .357 would be overkill. Thankfully, Florida is a gun friendly state for the good guys; guys like us."

"Good, keep 'em well oiled. No doubt we're goin' hunting on this one. We need to find this psychopath before he finds us or one of our family members. It'd be best for your daughter and her family to stay away from you for a bit. I'm doing the same with Cheryl and Hope. I made some calls. They'll be staying with my brother- and sister-in-law at their beach house. It might just be paranoia on my part, but with two dead, we can't take any chances."

"It never ends, does it, Mac?"

"We've got to stay positive. Hey, look at the bright side, Marty. This investigation will give you something to do between trips to the beach and the grandkids' birthday parties."

"That's a bright side I can do without, Bro."

8
AUGUST 11, 2015

3:47 PM
HAVANA, CUBA

On April 14, President Barack Obama announced that Cuba would be removed from the U.S. State Sponsor of Terrorism list. At that time, it was anticipated that business in Cuba would begin to flourish. It was not until December 17, however, that American businesses would no longer be barred from operating in Cuba. Cuban industries planned for expansion. With prospects of greater opportunities in the fabric industry, Maria Consuelo had her hopes high on finding a better paying job with less hours than where she'd been working. In August, however, the textile industry was fully staffed in anticipation of the upswing in sales. Plus, the work days were to grow longer with little additional pay. Dejected and tired from pounding the street on her day off, Maria decided to head home and give up her quest for finding a better job. Then she heard someone call out Maria!"

When she looked at the bus stop across the street, she saw the woman she spoke with a week ago.

"Over here!"

Maria crossed the street and walked to the bus stop.

"Remember me?" the woman said. "Vinita Garcia."

"Yes, yes, I do. Are you here all the time? The last time I spoke with you it was earlier, but the sun was still beating down."

"I come and go. I don't have a specific time looking for prospective clients. This was a lucky coincidence. Have you given it any thought about moving to America and working with friends of mine who pay very well?"

"I think I'll take you up on that. There's nothing here for me. No family, little money, and a job that will put me in an early grave."

"That's wonderful! I'm so happy for you. You won't be disappointed."

"What do I need for the trip? I only have a few pesos left."

"Just meet me here tonight at 9:30. There will be others making the trip with you. You'll have a place to stay with them by the boat. And don't worry about the money. I'll cover you. My friends can deduct what you owe me from you pay check or checks, depending how much you want deducted."

"How much will I owe you?"

"Just the original five hundred . . . and a twenty-peso finder/transaction fee."

"You said something the last time about interest."

"Forget it. You seem like a nice young lady. I'll waiver the loan interest. I'll still make money with the fee and commission. I just want you to be happy with the decision to start a new life. Now, don't forget. Be here 9:30 sharp."

4:09 PM
Sarasota, Florida

The basement smelled of underarm sweat. It was unfinished with only one light bulb situated in the center of the ceiling. Directly under the light were a bench, a chalk stand, and a power rack. Also located throughout the room were massive amounts of free weights, a dipping bar, rowing machine, and an inclined abdominal board. Unfortunately, there weren't any windows, exhaust fans, or vents to suck out the odor left by Alex "the Bull" Brisco, Jimmy "the Snake" Ramirez, and Dillon "Ripper" Campo; three ex-convicts who once lifted weights in the much more hospitable environment of the prison gym. Still, the basement of Ramirez's house was a place to meet, grow bigger and stronger, and to plot their next crimes.

"So, Bull, when's your next hit?"

"You'll know when it happens, Jimmy."

"You've been itching to square up with these two guys for a long, long time. You need Rip or me to help out, just say the word. You blew this last hit on Presler."

"How long have you known me," said Brisco. "I take care of my own problems. I'll take care of these two mutts in my own time and way. I'll have more opportunities to put a knife in Presler's chest or a bullet in his head. Then on to Taylor. Now shut up and load those plates on the bar. Today's the day I do five fifteen."

The bar was loaded.

Brisco stepped to the chalk stand. At age fifty-two, he was at his peak strength. He reached in and picked up the block of white powder. He rubbed it in his hands and dropped it back in the metal basin. He slapped his hands together causing a white cloud to fill the air around him. Brisco then snapped an ammonia capsule under his nose. He let out a grunt, sat on the bench which held the Olympic bar and massive amount of iron plates. This was his third attempt over as many days to break his previous bench press record of five hundred ten pounds. He laid back on the cushioned bench, widened his stance, brought his feet under his knees, and arched his back. Brisco reached for the bar above his head that held the quarter plus ton of iron. He slid his hands along the scored, chrome-steel bar until his index fingers found the circles indicating his grip had gone wide enough. Brisco squeezed the bar, then pulled himself off the bench. Arching his back further, he settled back onto the bench.

Campo and Ramirez stood at each side of the bench by Brisco's head, their hands cupped under the protruding ends of the Olympic bar.

Brisco nodded and the two men helped lift the weight off the racks. With the weight extended fully in his hands, he waited a full two seconds before lowering it to his chest. When the weight hit bottom, he strained every muscle in his body to put distance between his chest and the bar.

Brisco pushed hard with arms shaking. He slid his body back toward the bench ranks using his powerful leg muscles. The five hundred fifteen pounds came off his chest and continued to move ever so slowly. The bar began to sag on the left side before straightening back to parallel. Once the weight was about half way to a lock-out position, Brisco let out a grunt. He knew if he could get the weight off his chest and past his shoulders, his triceps would finish the lift. They were, after all, his strongest asset for the lift, surprisingly even stronger than his powerful chest muscles.

Brisco yelled just as he locked out on the weight. The spotters grabbed the bar and eased it back to the bench racks.

"Looking good, Bull," said Campo. "I guess those 'roids really kicked in today."

"Yeah, might be a good day to kill somebody, anybody."

"Are you serious?" asked Ramirez.

"Not quite ready yet to go on a killing spree. Not until I take out those two pigs, Presler and Taylor. Then my slate will be clean to deal with anyone who crosses us on our other businesses."

"Speaking of business," said Snake, "I know a guy who can make a lot of money for us. I did some work for him in the past. His name is Valverde, Benito Valverde. I don't know what happened, why he stopped calling me for jobs. Maybe it was the two new guys he hired. Anyway, now with your muscle we can ice those guys out. I can tell him that you're around and we can do business for him at a price he'd like. You want me to make the call?"

"Sure," said Brisco. "As long as it pays well, pays in cash, and is done in short order. Remember, I have some scores that need to be settled and I don't need any distractions."

4:44 PM
Bloomfield, New Jersey

"Do you have everything you need?" Mac asked Cheryl. "Jason, Ann, and the kids will be by soon to pick up you and Hope."

"Why can't I just take my car? I don't want to rely on them to take me everywhere."

"Because this guy Brisco might be around. I think he's still in Florida, but who knows? Even if he's not here, though, he might have several mutt friends floating around New Jersey. He or his gang of misfits might have IDed your car from an earlier drive-by and would be out looking for it. Let them think you're still here. I'll take care of business if any of them show up."

"I'm not liking this whole situation, Mac. This is not the environment I envisioned bringing up our daughter."

"I know. Who would have seen this coming? A guy I arrested thirty years ago is out and about looking to eliminate me and my family. Not to mention Marty and his family. Look, with two recent homicides connected to him, and as a target in the death of a DEA agent in Mexico, I suspect this nut case will be on a lot of PD radar screens. So, just sit tight for a while."

"Easy for you to say. You actually hope he shows up at our house."

"Not if you and Hope were here. Now, do you have everything you need/"

"I believe I do," she answered. "If not, you can bring whatever I forgot next week."

"That's if I'm not on a good lead," Mac said.

"Once again, the unfortunate consequences of your obsessive compulsions requiring us to rearrange our plans. Nonetheless, I'm looking forward to spending several days with my brother, Ann, and the kids down the shore for the summer. I know Hope is too."

"A year from now Hope will be in junior high. You won't be there for her like you have been at Washington Elementary."

"Maybe I'll see if there's a school nurse opening at Franklin. Nancy Crawford is getting up there in age. She might be retiring soon. I know I was lucky to get offered the school nurse job at Washington this year."

"Then again," Mac replied, "knowing Nancy, she'll be there until they throw her out. And as for Hope, leave the poor kid alone. She's almost a teenager. It's time she's out on her own, out from under mommy's wing."

"She's still my baby. You don't get it. Men don't understand the bond between mother and child. She will always be my baby, even when she's sixty . . . should I live long enough to see that day."

"I get it. Just don't smother her."

"Don't worry. I'll give her space. Well, I will when she leaves Washington behind and heads off to Franklin High."

Mac smiled. "Good. Now, as for me, I'll call when I can. Jason loves it down there in Lavallette. So, you'll have your brother to contend with, as well as your sister-in-law."

"Look, it's their shore house. Hope and I are just guests. Sun, surf, summer reading; that's it for us. We'll get along fine . . . for now. But this running and hiding has to stop, and soon. I want to live like normal people for a change. Get up, go to work, come home, and relax. You were a cop for many, many years. You handled these matters for the public. Why can't you just let the police take it from here?"

"Because this is personal. The target is on my back. Besides, I don't want you in anybody's crosshairs ever again. Particularly this maniac. Remember what I told you. This guy wants to take out me *and* Marty. And most likely our entire families. He's a sick bastard. He did thirty years in prison for raping the wife of a guy who owed him money. Now, like I said, two local homicides are attached to him: the husband of the rape victim and the eyewitness who saw him leaving the scene of the assault. I just don't want you near me for the next few days, at least. Hopefully, Marty and I will find this guy before he finds us."

"Then what? More of the same craziness. I still haven't gotten over when that other enemy of yours tried to kill me in our house when I was pregnant."

"Don't remind me. That's why I want you and Hope away from our house and with your brother and Ann. I'll be focusing on this sleazebag, Brisco. And I'm banking on the same fate for him as it was for Conroy."

"I've heard enough. Just be careful, and I pray this is the last confrontation you'll have with a homicidal maniac from your past."

5:30 PM

"M.C.T. Investigations"

"Mac, is that you? It's me, Roger Akins."

"Roger, I heard you left the Prosecutor's Office. How are things in the private sector?"

"Good, good. They trained me well in Essex County. Now that I learned all the ins and outs of the office, I can now defend those who need defending."

"You mean like your new clients' victims?"

Akins let out with a laugh. "Always thinking like a cop, Mac.

That's what I like about you. You're a P.I. now, though. Ever thought about working with the dark side?"

"I have and decided it's not my cup of tea. I know the perps you defend need a defense, but I'm not the one to help 'em with that."

"The money's the same color whichever side you're on," said Akins.

"Not how I see it," Mac replied. "Yours has a touch of red on it."

"My friend, I didn't call you to argue the merits of a defendant's right to counsel. And I'm sorry I'm calling so late. But I've just spent the last four hours with a new client. He has some very interesting information that I'm sure you'd like to know about. It involves your safety and the safety of your family, and Marty Presler and his family."

"What do you have, Roger?" Mac asked. "This is serious information?"

"Serious as a heart attack. I don't like to talk over the phone. Only God knows who's monitoring calls. I suspect you might even be taping this call. I know how you P.I.s operate. You can get away with 'one party knowing' tapes in New Jersey. So, let me be as cryptic as I can be over the air ."

Mac held the phone's receiver closer to his ear and broke in. "I'm listening."

"My client needs to talk with someone other than the police. He's not been arrested of any crime, and he's not being investigated of a crime. At least, not that I'm aware."

"Then what's the problem?"

"Can we come see you to explain the situation?"

"We?"

"Yeah, I'd like to be there with my client."

"Since this appears to be life-threatening information, let's do this asap. How's tomorrow, 9 AM?"

There was a pause as Akins checked his desk calendar. "I

have a 10 AM appointment. I'll cancel it. Considering travel time, we're going to need more than an hour. Besides, this needs to be addressed immediately. So, 9 AM is good."

Mac then gave Akins his home office address. "See you at 9," he said.

"Looking forward to it."

7:10 PM
Matanza, Cuba

Hurricane and tropical storm season in the Caribbean and Florida begins June 1 and ends November 30. Much of the hurricane and tropical storm activity in August of 2015, however, was taking place south of the Straits, by the Windward Islands. Due to the distance from the Straits to the northern areas of Venezuela and the Windward Islands, water in the 90 mile stretch between Cuba and the Florida Keys was relatively calm. *Good weather for boating,* Hector Jiminez thought.

Captain Jiminez's speedboat, La Halcón, sat at the dock along el Rio Canimar near the inlet to la Bahía de Matanzas, approximately twenty-six miles east of Havana. When let loose, the 40 foot, sixty-thousand-dollar boat owned by a Marielito crime family member could reach speeds close to 80 knots in the open sea. Today, however, La Halcón remained idle while Jiminez negotiated the piso (toll fee) for seven immigrants being trafficked into the United States via the river, the bay, and the Straits of Florida. The individual seated across from Jiminez was a local gang member. Not present, but wholly involved in the negotiations, was a government official representing a "nondisclosure" business for various intelligence officers in Cuba's Ministry of the Interior. It was agreed the five hundred pesos per immigrant toll fee would go to Captain Jiminez for his risk and troubles should he get caught along the way by members of the U.S. Coast Guard or Homeland Security. The six-thousand American dollar balance each immigrant was required to pay for the trip either had to be paid up front by the Cuban exile or by his/her family in the U.S. in order to have his/her loved one join them. U.S. government officials shy away from these prosecutions since they involve uniting family members.

Although travel rules began to change with President Obama and Secretary of State John Kerry, the smuggling business still prospered by cutting through all the red tape. The "wet foot, dry foot" rule still applied. Caught on the water, back to Cuba; make it to shore in the U.S., stay in the U.S.

Those individuals who could only afford the five-hundred-peso upfront fee would be required to work off their debt in the U.S. as laborers, housekeepers, factory workers, or sex workers. A fee that, in fact, would never be considered paid off. It was simply false hope offered by Jiminez on behalf of the U.S. and Cuban crime families, the Cuban Ministry of the Interior, and, at times, the Mexican cartels—members intent on trafficking those individuals indefinitely. Each immigrant was required to work off six-thousand U.S. dollars to pay for the trip . . . or so they were told.

"Okay," said Jiminez. "Look, Lucia tells me we might have one who can't come up with the initial five hundred. She has no relatives either here or at the other end, so I suspect even if she had the full six grand, you'd sell her off as soon as she hit land."

"That's right. We're not in the business of losing money. And as for Lucia, she's pretty reliable with the cash. She'll put up the five bills . . . and get it back double from her contacts in the Ministry. You just have to remember to call her by her cover name, Vinita, when you're around the cash cows."

"I know. I've dealt with her many times before."

"Just don't forget. She's been a big moneymaker for us," said the heavily tattooed, scar-faced man sitting across from Jiminez. "This is an easy one. We'll have Valverde's men jump right on that. We'll all do well with her. He'll pay two upfront for my people. We'll get the other four grand in short order once Valverde gets her working for him." He then added, "When are you plannin' to leave?"

"If all goes well and we continue with good weather, we'll leave early tomorrow morning, long before sunrise."

"You have all the bodies lined up?"

"Yes, according to Lucia."

"Vinita, don't slip."

"Yeah, yeah, Vinita. I'll be picking up the bodies in about two hours at a bus stop and bringing them here. They'll stay at the warehouse by the boat until we leave."

"Okay. We good?"

"We good."

The two shook hands and parted company.

9
AUGUST 12, 2015

2:33 AM
Matanza, Cuba
AND
Key West, Florida

The waves were mildly choppy, just under one foot high. La Halcón sat a bit heavy in the water from the extra-full fuel tanks for the trip back and from the weight of Jiminez and the passengers. Still, in spite of the added weight, the boat continued the steady run in good time, cutting through the water at half its full speed. The rocking caused several passengers to vomit over the side of the boat. Maria Consuelo was one of them. After about two hours, the speedboat carrying its Cuban refugees pulled within yards of the secluded Key West beach. The immigrants got out and waded to shore. Several vehicles waited to take them to Customs for processing as Cuban exiles seeking asylum. Family members who paid big money to the coyotes and drivers who brought their loved ones to the U.S. were to be waiting near the Customs and Border Protection Building upon thir arrival.

One vehicle's driver spotted Maria walking up the beach. He called for her to get in the back seat of his SUV.

"What about the others?" Maria asked, as she separated from the group, still wobbly from boat sickness. Then, staggering to the stranger's vehicle, she said, "Why are they all getting in other cars?"

"Just get in the back," said the man in the front passenger seat.

"How far to the Customs Office?" she asked, once inside the car. "I was told you were going to take me there once we reached shore."

"Don't you worry," said the driver. "We have to make one stop before we go there."

About an hour later, Maria asked again, this time a bit more nervous, "Where are you taking me?"

"Just shut up and sit back" was the response.

Several hours later, as the vehicle slowed at a traffic light just outside the city limits of Miami, Maria jumped from the car. She slipped, scrapping her knees on the pavement. She tried to distance herself from the SUV, but the male front-seat passenger was much quicker and stronger. As she tried to scream, he knocked her unconscious with a powerful right-handed fist. He quickly threw her over his shoulder and placed her back in the car. This time, though, he put a strip of duct tape over her mouth and wrists, effectively cuffing her around her back. He then pushed her down onto the floor between the front and back seats.

Approximately ten minutes later, Maria woke up. With tears in her eyes, she struggled to get up. The male in the front-seat passenger side reached over and pushed her down. "Now stay down, or I'll hit you again. Got it?!"

Maria felt lost, abandoned, and terrified the rest of the three-and-a-half-hour trip from Key West to an alleyway in downtown Miami.

It was hot, August hot in Miami, as the SUV edged its way down the alley. It stopped around back by a gray metal door.

"Get out and follow me," said the burly male from the passenger seat as he pulled her up by her bounded wrists.

The three entered through the metal door that belonged to the Latina strip club. Maria was escorted by the muscle down a back interior stairway to a windowless room with several single beds lined up against the walls. They were met by a tall, well-dressed male and female, two rather large men, and two young girls.

"Aah, thank you, gents," said the tall male to the driver and his companion. With eyes on Maria but addressed to her escorts, he added, "It looks like she gave you some trouble. I hope she has not been too mistreated." Then shaking his head and turning to the driver and his burly male passenger, he noted, "No matter. Just follow Maggie here; she'll walk you to a table by the dance floor and pay you for your services."

Turning toward Maria, the tall male said, "You, young lady, will be working for me." Looking at one of the men with him, he said, "Remove the tape from her mouth and around her wrists. We don't treat our girls like that. They are our work horses, but need to look like show horses. I don't want to see any marks on them. This will be the last time I'll use those two beasts for pickups and deliveries. I know one guy who was released from prison. He'll jump at transporting my girls." Then, with a laugh, he added, "And the price for shipping will be negotiable."

Now beginning to shake as the tape was removed from her mouth, Maria said, "Where am I?! Who are you, and why am I not being brought to Customs?!"

"Sorry you don't have any relatives waiting for you. Neither do these two runaway girls. So, I'm your family now. All three of you. You'll be working for me. If you try to leave at any time, you will be hunted down and hurt pretty badly, maybe even killed if I'm in that kind of mood that day. See these two large men here? They're going to make sure you don't leave this room. You'll be here for the night. Then you will be taken to one of my other businesses."

Maria ran toward the door. One of the men grabbed her and dragged her back to the far end of the room. "Try that again," said the tall male, "and you'll be working overtime at my massage-parlor in Orlando."

As the three men left the room and snapped in the padlock on the exterior side of the room, Maria and the young girls huddled together and cried.

Maria wiped the tears from her eyes. "In case we are separated or something very bad happens to one of us, let's remember each other's name."

The girls nodded in agreement.

"My name is Maria Consuelo Alvarez Rodriguez."

"I'm Jill Morgan."

"And I'm Maureen Sorbo.

9:00 AM
Bloomfield, New Jersey

A knock at the door.

"Come in," said Mac.

In walked two men. One man, the shorter of the two, was former Assistant Prosecutor Roger Akins. He was well-dressed; stock in trade for the vast majority of lawyers. Akins was just shy of five-nine. He had short brown, almost black hair and dark brown eyes. He was wearing a custom-made dark-gray suit with soft-leather, black wing-tipped shoes. He reached his hand out to Mac.

"Long time no see, Detective Sergeant Mac Taylor."

Mac shook Akins's hand. "No more detective sergeant, Roger. Now I'm simply P.I. Taylor, a title I'm happy to have after all the crap I've been through these last few years."

"In that case, Private Investigator Taylor, I'd like you to meet Alan Springer."

The young man was barely out of his teens. He was six feet in height, somewhat gawky looking. He was wearing a casual, knitted yellow-colored shirt and light-brown dress pants. He avoided eye contact as he shook Mac's hand.

"Good to meet you, Alan" was all Mac said before directing the two men to chairs by his desk. He then took out a pad and pen.

"So, Roger, what has your client here done that you think I might be of some help?"

Akins looked at the young man, then back to Taylor. "Well, Mac, in the vernacular, you might call Alan a computer hacker. You know how these young people are. They can do more with a computer in five minutes than we can do in five years . . . that's if we can do it at all. Alan made a big mistake recently. He might have broken the law, but that's a minor problem in the big scheme of things. You see, Alan had a girlfriend, Jean Debois, who he suspected was cheating on him. He, being the rambunctious young man that he is, decided to hack her email account to see who she was communicating with, and if there was another love interest in the picture." Akins turned to Springer. "Is that right, Alan?"

Springer nodded his head.

"He didn't find any interested paramours, but he did come across several emails from a guy to his ex-girlfriend, wanting information on Alan."

Akins continued. "The guy is an ex-con. He wanted the then-girlfriend to get in touch with him and help him find *you and Marty Presler*. When Alan did an in-depth background check on this guy, he came up with the name Alex Brisco. I did some research on my own. It brought me to that rape case you and Marty were on back in June of '85. This guy Brisco seems like a badass. I don't suspect he wants to find you two to play a game of golf."

"Why didn't you go to the police first with this information?"

"To protect my client and to give you a heads up. Alan here

could face various hacking charges by the police. We will go to them eventually, but I thought as a first option, you'd be the better choice. Plus, I'm sure you still have Marty's contact information. I thought you'd be the best one to bring him up to speed. If this guy Brisco wants you also, Alan won't stand much of a chance once he gives him the information. The police won't be able to protect him 24/7. Right now, they don't need to know how you came about this information. Like I said, we'll tell them eventually, but I have more faith you'll protect Alan than they will. You have a vested interest in finding Brisco first."

Mac looked at Springer. "Has Brisco contacted you yet?"

"Only once. I gave him the info he asked for: the phone numbers, addresses, and family members of Mr. Presler."

Mac shot a glance at Atkins. "What?!! And you want me to protect this snitch, Roger?!" Pushing his chair out behind him, Taylor rose and slammed both palms of his hands on his desk. "There are other homicides this dirtbag Brisco is suspected of committing." Pointing a finger at Springer, Mac said, "If your client here gave Brisco any info regarding those people, he's complicit in those murders. I should drag his ass down to the prosecutor's office right now. Luckily, Marty missed getting killed about a week ago by that river rat Brisco. But if he hadn't had luck on his side, you could've added another murder rap for abetting to your client here."

"Easy does it, cowboy. As soon as he told me what transpired between him and Brisco, I set up this meeting with the intention to warn you and Marty that this ex-con is after both of you."

Springer, looking at Atkins, said in a nervous voice, "Why'd you bring me here? I told you he wasn't going to like what I had to say."

"Relax, kid. I know you're not going to win any points with Investigator Taylor, but I suspect he will save your ass from jail and he will take this guy Brisco off your back. The police go on defense. They might catch him again and put him back in jail. Then again, they might not. In which case you'll be just another one of his targets. Just like those from his other case. Investigator Taylor, on the other hand, goes on offense." Then looking at Taylor, "Isn't that right, Mac? Need I say more?"

Mac sat back down. "No, enough said." Pointing at Springer but looking at Atkins, Mac added, "He'll be okay as long as he cooperates with me and Marty." Then, looking at Springer, he said, "Tell me, Mr. Hacker, what information do you have on Brisco?"

"Okay, okay. I did hack into Alex Brisco's credit-card records and found some places he's been in recently."

"This dirtbag has a credit card? He's been in jail for 30 years. How does anyone give him a card?"

"The banks don't care," said Springer. "The interest rates are so high on the cards that they'll give anyone an opportunity to owe them money. Besides, I suspect the application he submitted for the card might not have been completely accurate."

Then, pen and pad ready, Mac asked, "All right, tell me what you got on him."

Springer leaned forward. "Brisco's been spending money in and around Sarasota, Florida, lately. Before that, his EZ Pass records show he was recently in the NY-NJ area."

"Well, of course he's been in Sarasota. Marty Presler lives down that way. But you know that . . . because you gave Brisco that information! Fortunately, Marty is still alive. It looks like Brisco was there to kill him but for the grace of God was unable to complete his mission. And fortunately, I was able to warn him about Brisco yesterday."

"So, you were warned about Brisco before this meeting," said Atkins. "I'm glad to hear that."

"I know you're trying to rehab your client with me because of what he'd done giving out Marty's personal information, and before he gave him mine. You're lucky Marty's okay right now, as is his family." Then looking directly at Springer, Mac said, "If something happens to any of them, though, I will hold you personally responsible. And this is a warning from me, 'That's not a good place to be.'"

"He can make it up to you," Atkins said. "Let him work with you to find Brisco."

"This is just a guess, but I think he wants to kill me last because I was the one who put two bullets in him. I should have put one in his head. That would have saved a lot of people a lot of trouble. I suspect he wants me last so I suffer from the murders of all the others involved in his case."

With clasped hands, Mac swiveled back and forth in his chair. "Okay," he continued. "The info you just gave on his recent location in the New Jersey, New York area matches up with two homicides here, and his time in Florida coincides with the attempt on Marty's life. Opportunity, motive, and means. He meets all three criteria.

"Those records will be critical to those cases. The police need to know this, if they don't know already. The Florida location fits the bill; at least it does for me, that Marty did, in fact, have a brief encounter with Brisco on the beach. The police need to know that, too."

Atkins cut in. "I understand, Mac, but as you know hacking this info is illegal. Besides, I think it's probably due diligence for the police to run these checks on a suspect. If they did, I'm sure they'll reach out to you—oh, wait, the police already had. That's how you learned you were already on Brisco's hit list."

Mac brushed off the comment. With his chin resting on his hand, he looked at Springer, "What's the connection with your girlfriend and Brisco?" he asked.

"Ex-girlfriend."

"Okay, ex-girlfriend. What was the deal with Brisco?"

"He's a lot older than her. I remember her telling me her father served time with him in Trenton State Prison. They probably stayed in contact. Her dad, Mike Alfonso, must have told him that Jean was dating a computer hacker. That's why I think he wanted to meet with me."

Mac jotted down the names.

"Did you meet personally with him?"

"Once, at a diner in Nutley."

Akins jumped into the conversation. "I don't want Alan meeting with him again under any circumstances. As you know, the guy is a maniac. I know the police will want Alan to set up a meeting and have him go into that meeting. They'd want to wire him up. I don't want that. I know they will threaten him with criminal charges if he doesn't cooperate with them. I am very aware how this game is played. That's another reason why we are here today. My client will pay for your services to protect him. How you do that is your business. Just send me the bill."

"Well, first off, now that Marty and I are on Brisco's radar, I will need to know everything your client can dig up on him. I mean everything: where he lives; his friends; any family; where they live; what he's trafficking in; with whom he deals; names; addresses. I can go on, but you get the point. I will be in contact with him daily, maybe hourly until I get my hands on Brisco." Then looking at Springer, Mac said, "You understand what I'm saying? For the next several days, at least, I own you."

Springer nodded.

Mac then turned to Atkins. "I'll let Lieutenant Arnet know what I know. He doesn't need to know where the information came from or how it was obtained. I'll just tell him I've been snooping around, tapping all my contacts, the ones I keep close to my vest."

"Thanks, Mac. This is a tough one, I know. I'll be in touch." Atkins then gave him his business card and all of Alan Springer's personal information.

10:35 AM
Miami/Sarasota, Florida

Brisco's cell phone rang. "Hello."

"Yo, Bull, it's me, Benito Valverde, a friend of your buddy Snake. He told me you're out and about, and might be looking for work. I figured I'd give you a call. I might have a job for you. I got a package that needs to be delivered."

"Sounds good. Cash deal?"

"Of course."

"Snake told me all about you. He sez you pay well. Seems we can come to some sort of an agreement. Not on the phone, though. When and where do you want to meet?"

Valverde said, "Meet me in Miami tomorrow morning. It's a package deal. The package goes to Orlando. Snake knows the locations. Easy, peasy. Understand?"

Brisco wanted the deal, but he was a bit torn. "I was looking to take care of some personal business the next few days, but, okay, I'll put all that on the back burner. Cash comes first. Looks like that package delivery will only take a few hours to complete anyway."

"I need them to start making money for me. I need a little time to talk with them first, if you know what I mean. That should only take today. So, I'll see you tomorrow."

"Okay, I'll get to Miami sometime before noon. I should be at the other location by four or sooner."

"My girl Maggie will pay you what we agreed to when you get there with the package."

"How many in the package?"

"Three fish; one large, two small."

"I'll need company."

"Take Snake or Ripper. I don't care which one you take. Just get the package there on time. Whoever you bring with you is your business. His share of the delivery, though, is negotiable."

Brisco bit his lower lip. *Cheap bastard*, he thought to himself. Then out loud, he muttered, "All right, but his take won't be coming out of my pocket."

"Agreed. We'll talk when you get here," said Valverde before hanging up.

1:17 PM
Hackensack, New Jersey

Mac Taylor entered the Bergen County Homicide Squad and took a seat across from Lieutenant Arnet.

"Well, my friend, I didn't expect to see you so soon."

"Really? You were the one who gave me the heads up on Brisco. Do you think I'd just sit back and wait for something to happen?"

Arnet smiled. "How about a cup of coffee?"

"I'll pass . . . but thanks."

Arnet got up from behind his desk, walked over and closed the door to his office. "Okay, then, what'cha got?"

"I have information about Brisco."

"Great, great! Do you have a location on him?"

"Yep, he's in the Venice, Florida area."

"You sure? Where'd you get that info from?"

"From Marty Presler." Mac then leaned forward and told Arnet the conversation he had with Presler, regarding the beach incident, when he called to warn him about Brisco.

"Interesting." Arnet sat back. "Anything else?"

"Isn't that enough to contact the locals down there to be on the lookout for him?"

"Already done, Mac. We had traced his activities. We know, in general, his last known location was in the Sarasota area, which is just north of Venice, but we haven't zeroed in on an exact location yet."

"Did you ever think about letting Marty know?"

"To be honest with you, Mac, I really didn't know when Presler retired or where he might have moved to after retirement. I had no reason to. After all, he wasn't with my department, he wasn't a local Bergen County cop, and I had no dealing with him on 'the Job'. That's why I asked you to let him know about Brisco."

"Well, I'm going to save you some time, L.T. I bought a plane ticket to Sarasota. I'll be leaving tomorrow. Marty and I go way back. If Brisco is still there and he's looking to take Marty out, then that's where I'll be, with my buddy."

"I never doubted for a minute that you would inject yourself into this investigation. I understand you have a personal interest here. The scumbag might be planning to kill you as we speak. That's why I warned you about him. But, as a former police officer, you know I can't condone any civilian interference. And, right now, you are a civilian. A private investigator, I'll grant you that, but not a full-fledged member of the law enforcement community. Plus, you do work for defense attorneys and their clients from time to time. That Barrow-Darcy case, for one, sticks in my mind."

"Looks like that case helped put bars on *your* shoulders. I'm just surprised you weren't scooped up by the Feds because of it. They love guys like you. Image is everything in their organization." Mac got up and was ready to leave. Suddenly he turned. "Oh, by the way, since Brisco is in Florida, were you able to connect his travels with the two murders here in the New York, New Jersey area?"

Arnet let out a laugh. "You got some pair, Taylor! You pay me a left-handed compliment, then ask for information. Generally, I tell you to go pound salt. But I'm not going to, and I'll tell you why. I'll do it out of respect that you once carried a badge—I told you that once before. But more importantly, because you might actually find this bastard before he racks up more dead bodies. So, here's where we're at: we have records showing he was in the area when the murders occurred. We can prove that. We can prove that he had opportunity to commit the crimes. And we can show motive. Both victims helped to put him in prison. Those matters are not our problem right now. We need physical evidence, or eyewitness accounts, or even a snitch's statement tying Brisco directly to the murders. Our case against him, so far, is all circumstantial. If you can help move it into the slam-dunk category, I'm all ears. Call me if you find out anything useful."

"Okay. If I learn anything down in Florida, I'll let you know. There's one thing, though, that I'd like you to do for me."

With narrowed eyes, Arnet asked, "What's that?"

"Contact the Lavallette Detective Bureau. My wife and daughter are staying at her brother's shore house there. Have the PD keep a watch on the house for any suspicious activity while I'm away. If Brisco heads up this way, I don't want my family in his crosshairs."

Mac then handed Arnet a piece of paper with the Lavallette address and names of all the occupants.

"That I can do for you," said Arnet. "Now, go and enjoy Florida. And don't forget to send me a postcard."

Mac grinned. "Forget the *post* card. With some luck, I hope to send you back a *post* mortem report for Brisco."

"I didn't hear that," said Arnet as Mac was leaving his office.

1:25 PM
Sarasota, Florida

Entering the basement, Brisco said, "I just heard from Valverde."

"Something good?" said Ramirez.

"Everything okay, Bull?" asked Campo.

"Yeah, everything is fine. I'm a little pressed for time here. Snake, you were right. Valverde has a job for me. I have a pickup to make in Miami tomorrow. Three females—one adult, two teens, maybe pre-teens. I don't know. I won't be sure until I get there. I have to take them to his club in Orlando. I take it they might not want to go, so he told me I could bring another guy as muscle. I'm not sure how much he wants to pay, but it should be an easy ride. The girls will probably be drugged up."

"Whatever you need, Bull," said Campo.

"Well, I got another thing I want to have taken care of. Since I'll be busy with this job tomorrow, I need one of you guys to head north and find out what you can on that guy I told you about, Mac Taylor. And anything you can find out about his family. That would be a bonus."

"Where would Jimmy or me begin to look?" asked Campo.

"I have a Bloomfield address for Taylor, and an address for his wife's brother, a guy named Jason Strunella. You can begin there. Just let me know what you find out. I'm still working on how to take out Presler, so I'll have my hands full here for the next few days."

"If you want, I'll head north," said Campo. "I got family up there. It'll give me a reason to see one of my girls in Newark. Ramirez can go with you . . . if that's okay? After all, he's worked for this guy Valverde before."

"Agreed."

"Agreed."

"Time to get ripped," said Brisco as he reached into a corner cabinet of the room and pulled out a syringe and several vials of Deca-Durabolin. The three ex-cons proceeded to inject the steroid into their systems. After the juice kicked in, the three began a brutally harsh two-hour workout.

10

AUGUST 13, 2015

11:27 AM
Miami, Florida

Brisco and Ramirez pulled down the alleyway, to the back door of Amantes Latinas, the Cuban strip club in downtown Miami.

Brisco knocked on the back door.

"Yo, who's there?" came the response from inside the building.

"It's me Bull . . . and Snake. We're here to pick up the package."

The muscle opened the door and let them in.

"So, what we got?" asked Brisco.

"Three females. One in her thirties and two young girls, I think they're about sixteen each."

"I'm told we're to bring them to Valverde's club in Orlando."

"Yeah, to Chicas. You remember where that is? It's right off Route 4. You've got GPS, right?"

"Sure, no problem."

Brisco then asked, "What's the story with these girls?"

"The older one will be used for the bar or massages. The two chippies with be waitressing for a bit, before being put in his strip rotation, and probably later used as escorts. There's a lot to be made with these mangos, so don't screw up on the delivery. And be nice. The boss doesn't want to see any marks on them."

"What's their history?" asked Brisco. "Are there any missing-person cops or psycho relatives looking for them, who might get wind of their location? Not that we can't handle it. We'd just like to know, if that's the case."

"No. There shouldn't be a problem. Our gal in Cuba set the older one up. She thought she was going to get a seamstress's job in Miami. She has no relatives; no outside contacts. She was fronted the money to pay our guy in the boat. Maggie also took care of the driver, his partner, and our gal in Cuba after they dropped off the package."

"What about the young girls?"

"Both runaways from the area. They've been in town for a few days. One of our guys saw them on the street. He brought them to Benito and Maggie. Maggie offered them money, free drugs, and a modeling job. They bit, and here they are. One of our contacts in the PD checked if there were any missing-person alarms for them. He couldn't find any. Seems they both come from broken homes. You know the scenario: drug addicted, alcoholic parent; abusive boyfriend. Parents probably don't even know they're missing. Figured they're shacking up with someone. Less for them to worry about. These two are both high-school dropouts who like their dope. A pretty easy catch for us. We just have to get the girls out of the area. Get them to a less familiar place. You know the routine."

"Any of them going to be a problem on the way up?"

"Nope, we'll dope 'em up for the trip north. Just put them in the back of your van and throw a cover over them. You think you can handle it?"

"We can handle it. Just tell Valverde we expect a bonus for this delivery. If we get stopped, we're looking at kidnapping and trafficking offenses which entail long, long prison sentences, especially if you have priors, which we both do."

"I'll relay that message. Just don't get stopped," said the muscle with a smile.

"If we do, you can add cop murder to those charges."

Approximately one hour later, the heavily-sedated women were carried out the back door of the strip club, placed in Brisco's van, and covered with a canvas tarp. Brisco and company then headed north on a three-and-a-half-hour drive to Orlando's Cuban strip club, Chicas, Chicas, Chicas.

3:05 PM
Sarasota/Venice, Florida

"Marty, great to see you again," said Mac as he exited the Sarasota Airport.

"Too bad the reason for your visit couldn't have been different."

"I know. I wanted to get down here last night, but this afternoon flight was the earliest I could get."

"No matter, Mac. You're here now," said Marty Presler. "I'm so glad to see you."

The two got in Marty's car and headed down Route 75 to the Venice exit. From there, they headed west to Marty's house just north of the historic section of town.

"Nice place, Marty," Mac said as he got out of the car and walked past the palms and other tropical plants that lined the walkway leading to the front door of the one-story, Mexican villa-styled home.

"You did pretty well for yourself, old-timer."

"Look who's calling me an old-timer," said Presler. "You've got a year or two on me."

Mac laughed.

The two former Newark police officers then entered the house where Mac was brought to the spare bedroom.

"Here's where you'll be bunking for the next few days," Marty said. "With any luck we'll find this asshole Brisco before he finds us. Then we can relax over a beer and you can head back home to scenic North Jersey."

Mac's smile quickly faded as he contemplated what the next few days might bring.

"Yeah, we have to get this creep. I don't like leaving my wife and daughter with my brother-in-law to watch over them, but it looks like our boy is down here—from what you told me about that beach incident. And you know me, Marty. My first response has never been to go on defense. If he's still around looking to take *you* out, I believe our best move is to flush *him* out first. I've had time to think about this and I've come up with a plan. If you're on board with it, we can put the bait out starting tomorrow."

"All right," said Presler. "Let's go in the kitchen where you can lay out this 'plan' for me. Especially since I suspect I'll be the bait."

Mac and Marty went in the kitchen and sat down at the table.

"First order of business," said Mac. "I'll need one of your handguns for protection."

"No problem. What'd ya want, the .40 cal or the 9? I like to keep my .357. I'm still an old-school, wheel-gun kinda guy."

"I don't blame you. Can't go wrong with a revolver. I'll take the .40. You know me, Marty. If I have a choice, I'll always take the gun with the bigger punch."

"I see your point," said Presler. He then added, "Okay, the .40 cal it is. I'm not sure, though, Mac, how lending you one of my guns plays out here in the Sunshine State, but facing jailtime still beats laying in the morgue."

"Florida's a pretty good Second Amendment state from what I hear. I suspect I've got a better chance here in the courts taking out Brisco with *your* gun, than with *my* gun, under the same circumstances, within the Jersey legal system."

"I hear you, my brother. Hopefully, with a good plan, this whole deal with Brisco will go down smoothly." Smiling, as he crossed his fingers, Presler then said, "Now, my good man, what's your plan?"

"Okay, first tell me where would be a good place to meet Brisco."

3:45 PM
Sarasota, Florida
and
Verona, New Jersey

"Springer, it's me, Taylor."

"I was expecting you to call me sooner," said Alan Springer. "Can I go about my business now? Has everything been taken care of?"

"Not yet. Here's the deal. I need you to get in touch with Brisco."

"What?! Oh, no! He's still around? I thought you just wanted me to get info on him . . . which you never did call me about. I thought I wouldn't have to deal with him again. I really don't like doing that. I don't think my attorney would want me to do that, either. It was my understanding I was only going to reach out to *you* if he called me."

"Listen to me," said Mac. "Just do what I say. I've been way too busy to call. But now I need *you* to make a call, to call Brisco. You hacked into private records and gave them to a hitman who wants to kill me and my buddy. You might have even abetted him in the killing of two people up by you. Now, do what I ask or get ready for overnight stays at the county jail."

"What two people killed 'up by me'?"

"Ask Roger. Your attorney is aware of the deaths."

"I had nothing to do with anyone being killed."

"You can tell that to the cops when they come to arrest you. Now, are you going to do what I'm telling you to do?"

"Okay, what is it you want me 'to do'?"

"Simple. I want you to contact Brisco. I want you to tell him you found out some interesting information on where Martin Presler likes to hang out."

"That's it? Between you and me, I already told him about places he'd likely go to fish, swim, play golf, lay in the sand."

"Oh, so you told Brisco how Marty liked to go to the beach."

Mac said it loud enough for Presler to hear that part of the phone conversation. Looking at Marty, he pointed at the phone, then made a throat-slitting move with his left hand.

"He just wanted to know where Martin Presler would go to relax."

"And you had no problem giving him that information?"

"I don't even know who Martin Presler is, nor did I know why Brisco wanted the information. All I did know was that Brisco was an ex-con who promised to hurt me if I didn't help him."

"Okay, back on track, this is what I want you to do. Contact Brisco. Tell him you knew he was interested in knowing Martin Presler's whereabouts. So, you hacked into his cell phone and learned some things that Brisco might be interested in knowing. When he bites, tell him that Presler will be meeting a friend out by the jetty just north of downtown Venice, tomorrow at 12 noon. Are you writing this down?"

"I can't hack into someone's cell phone."

"That doesn't matter. He doesn't know that. Just tell him you hacked into something else then; his emails, for example. I really don't think he'd know the difference. Just do it. Tell him Martin Presler will be meeting a friend by the Venice jetty tomorrow at noon."

"Okay, okay."

"That's not all, though. I want you to run a license and vehicle check on Alex Brisco. I know the address won't be much of a help right now, but I need to know what he might be driving."

"Well, I can tell you that right now," said Springer. "Give me a minute."

A few minutes later, Springer said, "Brisco has a New Jersey driver's license and Newark address. He has a Jersey registered vehicle; a blue 2012, Ford van." He then gave Mac the license plate number.

"Okay, here's your job for the next two days," said Mac. "Run everything you have on Alex Brisco—locations, friends and associates, organized crime connections—I mean everything. I'm particularly interested in his movements. Don't give him any info on my whereabouts, my family's whereabouts, or Marty Presler's family's whereabouts. Right now, the only info you are to tell Brisco is where Martin Presler will be at noon tomorrow. Got it?!"

"Yeah, is that it?"

"That's it for now."

4:07 PM
ORLANDO, FLORIDA

Chicas, Chicas, Chicas was your typical strip club—elevated dance floor having several brass poles running from floor to ceiling. An elongated, oval bar encircled the elevated dance floor. Stools lined the bar and private booths ran along the walls. An aisle between the stools and the booths allowed for the topless, young waitresses to take orders from the predominately older male customers. The windowless room was lit with a strobe light above the dance floor, several top hats over the bar area, and floodlights in the corners of the room. The corner areas remained mostly dark for privacy, but when the room got quite busy with customers, the floodlights were turned on. They would throw out yellowish-red rays of light that would pulsate to piped-in music. Unlike its North American strip-club cousins, though, the piped-in music at Chicas was mostly a mix of Cuban, Latin American and West African music. The semi-naked Latinas who danced and waitressed would take tips from the customers. At the end of the night, those tips would be turned in to the lady of the house: Señora Maglia, aka Maggie Hernández Selina.

Maggie Selina and Benito Valverde were seated in one of the dark corners of the room.

"Did you pay Brisco?" asked Valverde.

"Yes, with yesterday's bar and tip money from the girls," said Maggie.

"Did you take our cut first?"

"Yes, of course."

"Good. You deserve your share for keeping the girls busy. I'll check later in the safe to make sure my share is in there."

"Of course it is! Why do you question me? You know I wouldn't short you. In fact, I've made a lot of money for you over the last few years. These girls need to eat, have clothes, medical care if necessary . . . and they have to stay in line. I do that for you. It comes out of my take."

Valverde nodded, then asked, "How are those new girls doing?"

"Okay," replied Maggie. "I don't know if the young ones are ready yet to go out on the dance floor. They need a little more coaxing."

"Put 'em topless waitressing, then. They can't screw up there. They don't need to be professional floor walkers."

"One of the girls keeps crying. We can't have that here. She needs to be broken. We're not babysitters. She needs to work . . . and work soon. Otherwise, send her back to Miami and put her in your parlor there where at least you'll get some trick money out of her."

Valverde let out a groan. "All right, I'll have Brisco and his buddy pay her a visit. I hear he's a take-no-prisoners kind of guy. He did time for rape. I suspect he'd enjoy breaking our noncompliant ones."

"Well, he needs to do whatever he does best, soon," said Maggie. "This girl needs to start making money for us."

"Put the other one on the floor. If she gives you any trouble, I'll have Brisco deal with her, too."

"One more problem, Benito."

"What now?"

"The older one's called Maria. I can put her on the escort list but I think she'll need a little coaxing, too. We can't threaten her with going after her family 'cause she has none. And she might not be so easily intimated with physical threats. I'm not sure how she'll be broken down. I'm not sure your boy Brisco would be the answer there. Let's put her behind the bar for the time being. The girls behind the bar aren't topless. Besides, it's a juice bar so she doesn't need to be an expert mixologist."

"Well, worse-case scenario, we send her into the S&M community. We can make some money off her there. Brisco might be able to help, too; but knowing that nut bag, he might just kill her. What a waste that would be, in time and money."

Just then, the front door to the club opened and a stream of white light poured in. In walked two Hispanic males in their thirties. They pulled out two stools from the bar in close proximity to Selina and Valverde and sat down.

"Two OJs," said Carlos Sanchez.

"And take it out of here," said Ryan Cabrero as he threw down a fifty-dollar bill.

Carlos Sanchez and Ryan Cabrero didn't just drop in on a work break. They *were* working. Sanchez and Cabrero were federal workers. ICE agents, to be exact, assigned to the Department of Homeland Security's Center for Countering Human Trafficking.

4:30 PM
Verona, New Jersey
and
Sarasota, Florida

"Hi, Mr. Brisco. It's me Alan, Alan Springer."

"Funny you should call. I was just thinking about our last conversation."

"How's that?"

"Well," said Brisco, "I wanted to know if you had gotten any more information on Taylor and Presler."

"Actually, that's why I was calling."

"Really now. And you want to help me look for them because . . . ?"

"Because I figured the sooner you locate them, the sooner you'll stop calling me for information. Then, I can go back to my normal life."

"Sure thing. So, what-a-ya got?"

"I was able to tap into Presler's cell phone, and I found out where he's going to be tomorrow at 12 noon."

"And where might that be?"

"It's out by a jetty, just north of downtown Venice."

"And why would he be there?"

"He's going to meet a friend. There's a restaurant there. I guess they're going to meet for lunch."

"Who's the friend?"

"I don't know. I was able to tap into the call, but I couldn't get a register on the caller's number. Though no names were exchanged in the conversation, the caller had a man's voice. That's the best I can do."

"Okay," said Brisco. He then asked, "Is Presler still driving the same car?"

"Looks that way. No motor vehicle record changes that I can see."

6:00 PM
Lavallette, New Jersey

Jason Strunella sat on a bench by the entryway to Lavallette Beach. He was wearing a pair of swim trunks and a buttoned-down island shirt. Under the shirt was a shoulder holster that held his .380 APC handgun. His eyes were fixed on his sister and his niece. Jason promised Mac that he would keep them in his sights when he could, whether they were aware of it or not. He also needed to keep watch on his own wife and kids who were presently building a large sand castle with Cheryl and Hope. Not knowing how deep this enemy of Mac's was willing to go, he was itching to get back to the beach house where the family would, at least, have the protection of locked doors and an alarm system.

Jason stood and scanned the beach from Ocean Unit 3 on the north shore to the Seaside Heights Boardwalk in the south, looking for anyone appearing out of place. *Nothing to report to Mac so far*, he thought.

As the sun continued on its path west, the sky directly above the sunbathers became a richer blue, the sand a more golden brown, and the eastern horizon a steely gray. Jason enjoyed being *at* the beach this time of day; just not *on* this day, under these circumstances. Though early evenings on Lavallette Beach generally conjured up warm, tranquil feelings for him, that was not the case today. The fear of an enemy lurking under each umbrella loomed large in his mind.

Jason wasn't a big fan of all aspects of beach life, however. In contrast to the serene beauty of the early evening sun, the Atlantic Ocean was a powerful force to be reckoned with. It was beautiful, yet deadly. Very deadly. Jason understood both its natures. It looked very tame at low tide. Bathers could float between a sand bar and the shore, or take leisurely swims farther out. But at high tide, waves crash onto the beach like the descending hammer of Thor. Adding to the brutal pounding of waves, riptides cut sharply along the shore's drop-off points, creating powerful undertows. *If that isn't enough*, Jason thought, *there are a whole bunch of sea creatures that won't hesitate to kill you. Not much different from the human predators that walk on land.*

"Cheryl!" Jason called out.

She turned upon hearing his voice and noticed him standing farther back along the beach. She waved to him. Then turning toward Hope, she said, "Time to go."

"Can't we stay just a little bit longer?" asked Hope.

"No, Uncle Jason is calling us. It's getting late. Time for dinner. Besides, you won't be going in the water anymore today. The water is just too rough."

"What about our sand castle, Mom? Will it be here tomorrow?"

"I don't know, honey. Maybe. It seems far enough back that high tide won't wash it away. If it does, just build another one tomorrow."

"I don't want to build another one. I want this one."

"Well, there are just some things we have to leave to faith. If it's meant to be, it'll be here tomorrow. In the meantime, get all your stuff together, we're heading back to Uncle Jason and Auntie Ann's place."

11

AUGUST 14, 2015

9:05 AM
BLOOMFIELD, NEW JERSEY

"There's a truck and car in the driveway at Taylor's place, but this place is dead," said Campo into the phone.

"Did you check Strunella's house?"

"Yeah. One car in the driveway. No activity there, either. Bull, I sat on both houses, on and off, for most of the night. No one going in, no one coming out. No lights on at either place."

"You sure you got the right places?"

"I went to the addresses you gave me. Maybe your info is wrong. Or maybe they got wind that you're looking for them and they left town."

Brisco mulled that over in his head for a moment before replying. "Well, stay up there for now. I got business to take care of down here. If they left town, I got a guy who might know where they went. If you find out anything, call me. Don't move on the info. Just call me. Okay?"

"Sure thing. And staying here for a while works for me. I got my girl in Newark. I'll bed down with her. But I'll be square with you, Briz, I don't know what info I'm gonna get for you. With nobody at either house, I'm at a dead end here."

"Just stay put, okay? I'll send you whatever info I can drum up. I just need you to be my eyes and ears up there for now. I want to limit how much time I'm in that neighborhood. They might be looking for me up there. You know what that's all about."

"Yeah, I gotcha," said Campo. "Lay low. Maybe I can get something for you within the next few days."

"I hope to clear up one account shortly. Laying low is not an option. After my meeting this afternoon, I'll be heading north to take care of that other matter."

11:58 AM
Venice, Florida

The Venice jetty is a narrow strip of concrete, bordered by large rocks. It extends approximately a football field in length alongside the inlet to the Gulf. It's a hot spot for fishermen and tourists. There's a restaurant to the east of it and a border of rocks protecting the shoreline to its left. Just east of the rocks is an unpaved parking lot that is prone to flooding during the rainy/hurricane season. To get to the jetty parking lot, one must head to Venice Beach, make a right turn at the end, pass the marina, and look for the open space. Since August is not a busy season for Venice, there is usually an ample number of parking spaces available. Today was no exception. In fact, there were fewer cars there today than usual. Counting Marty Presler's car, there were seven in all. One of the other cars was a 2014 white Toyota Camry.

A blue Ford van slowly entered the parking lot. The driver rolled down the passenger-side window and stopped perpendicular to the back of Presler's car. It's operator, Alex Brisco, picked up the loaded shotgun off the passenger seat of his vehicle, aimed the weapon at the back of the driver's head, and fired one round of a rifle slug through the back window. As the head of the driver exploded, Brisco pumped three more 12-gauge rounds through the shattered back window.

While Brisco was squeezing off rounds into Presler's car, the white Camry burned rubber to get alongside his van. At the same time, a gray Chevy sedan raced into the parking lot. Brisco looked to his left and saw the front and back passenger-side windows of the Camry down and two guys, the driver and a guy in the back seat, with guns aimed at him. He ducked and stepped on the gas as Presler and Taylor unloaded their weapons into his van. One bullet grazed Brisco's right hand causing him to jerk the steering wheel to the left. His van fishtailed to the right before heading out of the lot. Mac turned to follow but was cut off by the gray Chevy sedan.

"Police!! Police!! Out of the car!! Drop your weapons!!" yelled Carlos Sanchez as he crouched down by the front of his car, exposed badge in one hand, gun aimed directly at Mac with the other.

"Hands up!! Hands up!!" chimed in Cabrero who moved to the rear of the car with a chained badge now around his neck and his gun pointed at Presler.

"Are you kidding?!" Mac said in frustration. "You're letting him get away!"

"Hands up! Hands!"

"Okay, okay," said Presler. "We'd better do it. We're in their ballpark now."

Mac and Marty were cuffed and read their rights. Cabrero then called the Venice Police to handle the scene. While they waited for the locals to respond, the ICE agents learned that Mac and Marty were targets of Alex Brisco. It was then that Mac and Marty learned that Sanchez and Cabrero had Brisco on their radar. They were tailing him when they heard the gunshots.

"We know Brisco and where to find him. We didn't know you guys, though. Besides, we didn't see him shoot up your car. We only saw you guys firing away. Granted, we're a little more free-spirited down here, but it still isn't the wild west. You just don't go unloading your weapons in public."

"Did you see what Brisco did to Marty's car and the mannequin in the front seat?" asked Mac.

"Listen, we'll let Venice PD process the scene," said Sanchez, "while you guys come with us to their headquarters. Our office is a bit too far away to head down there. Besides, there's a lot of local issues that have to be dealt here, like attempted murder, conspiracy to commit murder, discharging firearms in public. The local DA will be adding more charges, I'm sure. There's a lot here that needs to be digested. In the meantime, I'll recommend our office or the locals put out an APB on Brisco and his vehicle. It's a hot-pursuit issue right now, so a patrol unit might just grab him while we head back to the PD."

"You'd better emphasis, in caps, 'armed and dangerous!' The guy was out to kill me! He'll kill anyone who tries to stop him. You should have just let us run him down," said Presler.

"I don't know how it was done back in your day, old-timer, but unfortunately, that's not the way we do business in 2015."

Presler just looked at Mac and shook his head mumbling "old-timer" under his breath.

12:09 PM
Venice Municipal Airport, Florida

"Snake, it's me," said Brisco out of breath.

"What's up?"

"I've been set up! That's what's up! Presler's on to me. Springer is now on my hit list. I'll explain later. Right now, though, I need you to come get me. I left my van at the Venice Airport, and I'm across the street by a restaurant called Sharky's. Hurry! Get here quick. The cops are after me! I'll explain when you get here. I'll be laying low by the restaurant or out by the pier behind it, if there's enough people out there to give me cover. I've got my hand wrapped in the front of my shirt. The asshole I was after landed a shot at me. Not serious but some blood on me and in the van. Just hurry up and get here. Call me when you're getting close. I'll look for your car. Hurry!"

"Hang tight. I'm about a half-hour away. Get as far away from that stolen van as you can. Once the cops locate it, they'll saturate that area. Sharky's and that pier would be the first place they'd look. There's a beach section just north of the restaurant. Head that way. You'll see what I'm talkin' about. You'll see a small parking lot. There are bathrooms, raised picnic platforms, and a lot of brush in that area. The bathrooms are a bit secluded. Might be a good place to duck into. It might buy you more time. I'll meet you there. I won't call until I get in the lot. Hide in the woods, if need be, till I get there. I'll loop around by the bathroom and pick you up."

12:27 PM
Venice Police Department, Florida

"You can all have a seat in here in the conference room," said Venice Detective Sergeant John McDaniel.

Sanchez and Cabrero offered their thanks as they led Mac Taylor and Martin Presler into the room. All four sat around the long, metal table.

"Please join us," Sanchez said to McDaniel who had all intentions of doing so. After all, he knew that he would be inheriting this case from a local standpoint, and it looked, on its face, that there was going to be a lot of local legwork to be accomplished.

Mac and Marty were again given their Miranda Warnings, orally. They were then given a Constitutional Rights form to read, check off, and sign that they understood their rights.

"Funny being on this side of the table," said Marty. "Especially after all those years of service we gave to the Blue."

McDaniel took the written documents and placed them on a filing cabinet near him.

Sanchez looked over at Cabrero. "Go ahead, Ryan, start the ball rolling."

"Okay," he said as he tapped his fingers on the table. "Now, tell us what the hell is going on that caused you two to cause havoc in this tranquil Floridian town? And don't give us the Reader's Digest version. We want to hear the whole nine yards. That is, if you want us to help provide any defense with the powers to be for your actions. Let's start with you, Mr. Mac Taylor."

"Well, whether you like it or not, I'll give you the 'Reader's Digest' version first, to save time. Then I can go into the longer version so you can give Brisco more time to disappear."

"Enough with the wisecracks," said Cabrero. "Stop wasting time. Your story, what is it?"

"Simple. Marty and I arrested Alex Brisco back in 1983 for kidnapping, rape, and attempted assault on a police officer. I put two bullets in him at the time. Since then, he was released from prison. Following his release, the husband of the victim and the witness in his case had been murdered. Brisco is the prime suspect in both murders. Lieutenant Arnet of the Bergen County Prosecutor's Office Homicide Squad in New Jersey said Marty and I—and possibly our family members—are likely to be his next targets. I'll let Marty take it from there."

"A few days ago, I was at Caspersen Beach waiting for my daughter and her family to arrive. A guy with a towel over his hand and arm started to approach me but limped away when my daughter and her family got closer. I don't know why he suddenly turned and left. From a cop's point of view, something just didn't seem right about it. Then, when Mac told me about Brisco's release and that he still had a noticeable limp from the bullets he took the day we arrested him, I figured that was a hit attempt by him that for whatever reason didn't go off as he planned. I wasn't about to give him a second chance."

"Neither was I," said Mac. "That's why I'm here right now. If we go down, Brisco's going with us. You've seen what he did to Marty's car. Look, if you want all the back story on this guy Brisco, call Lieutenant Arnet in Bergen County, New Jersey, and he can fill your case jacket with a wealth of information. Now I've got one question if I might ask."

"Go ahead," said Cabrero. "I don't know if I can answer it, but you can ask."

"Why were you here today out by the jetty? I suspect you've had Brisco on your radar for some reason. Did you let Arnet know? He's been looking for him. He put out bulletins for the guy. I know you Feds work on a whole different way of conducting business. For example, if you have him in your playbook, either as a snitch or steppingstone to get at a higher up, you're not about to give him up. I don't know that to be the case, but I've been around the block a few times, and I know how this game is played."

"Well, you're right about one thing," said Cabrero. "We were keeping an eyeball on Brisco. But we are not yet prepared to tell you anything else about our interest in him. We are here to get information from you two, not the other way around."

"Even though we're two former cops whose lives and our families' lives are at stake? You don't want to help?"

"Okay, I'll give you this. You ever hear of 'go-fast boats'?"

"Go on," said Presler.

"Well, occasionally the Coast Guard grabs one that sneaks illegal aliens into the country from Caribbean nations to the Florida coast. When they catch one, they turn the occupants over to us. We interrogate them and sometimes we get some good information.

We can be persuasive. We have many tools in our chest. I'll give you this," said Cabrero. "Brisco's name came up as a player in the trafficking business. And that's *our* business. We want to know who he's dealing with. That's why we were at the jetty today."

McDaniel was just called out of the room. A few minutes later he returned.

"We just got information that we found Brisco's van," said McDaniel. "It was dumped by the airport."

"How about Brisco?" asked Sanchez.

"No luck there. But there was a shotgun found in the front seat. Our guys dusted the gun and van for prints. An AFIS check on the gunprints came back to Brisco. His prints were also located throughout the van. Two other sets of prints came back positive for two ex-cons: James Ramirez and Dillon Campos. We'll be following up on those two as well as Brisco."

Mac peered over at Presler, then directly back at Sanchez. "Looks like *you* have two good leads."

"Yeah, *our* leads. Don't get any ideas about leapfrogging over us. We are going to handle this, methodically. We don't want any problem with the courts. We'll get the information we need from these ex-cons one way or another but legally. We don't plan on shooting our way through this. Understand, gentlemen?"

"Absolutely," said Presler.

Mac just hunched his shoulders and nodded.

12
AUGUST 15, 2015

8:15 AM
ORLANDO, FLORIDA

At the strip club, Brisco and Ramirez began shooting up a quantity of steroids.

Brisco sat back on the bed and shook his head. "Springer set me up. That punk will pay."

"How do you know that? And, if he did, *why* would he do it? He should know better than to cross you."

"Well for one, he gave me the location where Presler was going to be and the car he was going to be in. And two, I got a quick look at one of the guys who pulled up and took a shot at me, I think it was Presler. I hadn't seen him in years, but he sure looked like the guy on the beach, the one I should have killed that day. If that was the case, if it was Presler, he knew what was going down and he was ready for it. Fortunately, I hit the gas a split second before he fired. Otherwise, I wouldn't be here right now."

Ramirez scratched his head, "But you said you shot someone in the car. Who was it, if not Presler?"

"I have no idea."

"Then how could that be a set up? I don't think that cop would put someone in that position if he knew what was going down."

"Who knows what that mutt would do? Maybe whoever was in the car was a decoy and Presler didn't think I'd come out shooting. I don't know. Something about that whole incident just doesn't make sense. Why, for example, did some car stop the shooters from following me? Maybe they were 'good citizens' who heard all the commotion and just wanted to get involved. Maybe they were a surveillance team following Presler and company . . . or worse yet, following me! Whatever the case, they did me a favor, though I still haven't figured out why. Something just stinks about this whole thing. But the fact remains that Presler seemed to have been given a heads up. And that means one of two things; either Springer is working both ends now or his line is being tapped and the cops know every one of our conversations. In either event, Springer is history. He has to be taken care of. I don't know just how I'm going to play that one . . . yet."

"Man, your list keeps getting longer. Forget Springer. Right now, it looks like you're oh for two with Presler. And now, if he's on to you, it's going to get much harder to put him away."

Brisco gave a hard look at Rameriz. "Don't you worry about my odds with him. What's the saying? 'Third time's the charm.' I had the edge the first time. I should have acted and taken him and his family out. Missed opportunity. Granted, he had the edge the second time, but fortunately I was able to bail out of there before he landed any shots. So now, we both know the game. The good news is he's got to be worried. He knows I'm coming for him, but he doesn't know how or when. Unfortunately, I'm down one car *and* I need more time to square up with him. Right now, though, my main goal is to get out of this hell hole."

"Well, good luck with that. Call me if you need me."

The two shook hands.

"I suspect I will need you . . . and soon," Brisco said with a smile.

He then dropped down from the twin bed in the back room

of Chicas and pumped out a hundred push-ups and one hundred sit-ups.

8:42 AM
Orlando, Florida

In walked Benito Valverde.

"Where's Snake?"

"He left about a half-hour ago, back to his place in Sarasota."

"So, what's your plan, now that every freakin' cop in Florida is looking for you?"

"I need to stay down low. And I need your help. I know what you're thinking. How much help and how much is it going to cost. Rest assured, I can come up with cash in exchange for help getting the hell out of here."

"That's good to know 'cause you're not staying here," Valverde said. "You're too hot for business. I want you out of here."

"I don't want to be here! But you want to throw me out?! That's rich. I need to lay low for a while. I can't stay with Snake. I need to distance myself from him right now. I need your help. I need a safer place to stay than this jiggle joint, anyway. You want me out in the street? When *you* needed me, I was there for you. But now that things are reversed, it's a different story!"

"You did one job for me. I don't owe you a thing! Besides, you're a loose cannon. Before this shit hit the fan, I was going to have you handle a little problem for me. Good money for you. Now that's all out the window, 'cause you went and shot up a car in broad daylight in Venice. Now I know how you got your handle. You're a bull in a China shop."

"I had a score to take care of. Someone crosses me, all hell's gonna come down on them,'"

"Yeah, well, a little common sense never hurt. You had a score to take care of? How'd that work out for you? I planned on using you to do some real nasty work in my business, and you were going to get paid well for it. But you are radioactive. I don't need the heat coming around. I need you out of here! Comprende, Bull?"

Brisco was raging inside from the steroids. "Okay, you want to play it that way, we'll play it that way," he said. After realizing he still needed Valverde to help him get out of town safely, he switched gears. "And what's this little problem you wanted me to take care of?"

Valverde had his muscle close the door of the back room. "I have two girls who need attitude adjustments. That's right up your alley, but it looks like that's to be put off for the time being. I'll have my guys handle it. I heard about your reputation for rape and murder. My guys might not be so persuasive as you, but the job will get done without all the fanfare you seem to attract."

"I can take care of business here, if you want, before you arrange to get me a gun, ammo, and set of wheels. Are the girls still here?"

"Oh, now you want a gun, ammo, *and* a car!"

"I need some protection. Can you do it? I can work over the girls as payment."

"Forget the girls. The car, gun, and ammo are going to cost you, big time. That's a price tag I need to think about. I want you out of here asap. I don't need any cops showing up, asking questions. Besides, you'll be safer if you head out of state."

"You'd think so," said Brisco. "I'm not so sure. I'll head north to take care of some other business. Not a good look, though. The cops up there must also be looking for me. I dropped two bodies in their backyard. They must've connected those killings with my old case. I don't think I left any evidence to attach me to the killings, but I still have to be on their target list . . . probably numero uno. So, although it might be less hot up there than it is here—and I'm not talking about the weather—I still gotta stay on the down low."

"Man, you attract cops like flies to shit," said Valverde pointing a finger at Brisco. "I'll help you this one time, and this one time only. But it's gonna cost you."

Brisco thought to himself, *this list of mine might just be getting longer.*

9:00 AM
VENICE POLICE DEPARTMENT, FLORIDA

"You two are cleared to go," said Detective Sergeant McDaniel. "Your buddies, Sanchez and Cabrero, put in a good word for you with the DA. Our 'stand your ground' legislation allows you to defend yourself. It mostly pertains to your home, yard, and workplace, but it also includes your car. How the Castle Doctrine applies here is quite a stretch; but since you were initial targets of Brisco, since your car was shot up by him, and since he was an imminent threat to you two in your rental car, you've both been given a green light to leave. And that's taking into account that both handguns were registered to you, Martin, and were used in self-defense. Our report won't be ready for a couple of days. You can tell that to the insurance company and rental car agency. They will definitely need a full report on how the damages occurred to the vehicle. Not your standard damage report."

"Thanks, detective," said Presler.

"Appreciated," added Taylor.

"There's one issue, though, that doesn't sit well with my bosses. Why wasn't anyone in my department notified of what was going to transpire at the jetty? You guys knew Brisco was going to be there. You set him up. If we were notified, he'd be in the can as we speak. We would have had that whole area covered."

It was Mac who spoke first. "Brisco's not a novice. He'd pick up on any surveillance car in the area. We didn't want to take the chance of spooking him."

"Well, that's not entirely true. Sanchez and Cabrero had him under surveillance, and he didn't know it."

"Yeah, one car; not several unmarked units. Look, he backed off at the beach when he had an open shot to kill me, for whatever reason," added Presler. "We didn't want him to back off again. We don't know how many chances we'd have to catch him."

"You mean *kill* him. I'm not stupid. That's what this is all about. You guys don't want him caught. You want him dead."

"I wouldn't have lost any sleep if he took a few shots to the head," Mac said. "As it is, he wasn't killed and he wasn't caught. So, I guess we're back to square one." He then asked, "If you don't mind, have you got any leads in the last twenty plus hours on where Brisco might be?"

"Man, you are persistent. You'd think, you'd be happy just getting out of here without charges."

"Look, Detective McDaniel . . ."

"You can call me John."

"Okay, John," said Mac. "Marty and I aren't the only ones this dirtbag Brisco is after. Our families are also on his chopping block. So, we need any information we can get our hands on, and as quickly as we can get it. What you are doing for us is more than a brother-in-blue courtesy, it could save lives. After all, isn't that what we're in business for?"

"Yes, and other things . . . like protecting sources and data," said McDaniel. "But, okay I'll give you some inside info. Hopefully, it'll help you guys from getting your asses blown away by this miserable bastard. Use the information wisely.

"First off, the shotgun had been stolen in a home invasion in Miami. The husband was beaten to the inch of his life and his girlfriend was raped."

"Boy, if that doesn't sound like Brisco," said Presler. "Up to his old tricks."

"Miami PD put out a composite drawing, based on what the husband told them at the time, which surely looked like Brisco. After we notified Miami that the shotgun was in his possession, they put together a photo array with him and five other ex-cons. The husband picked Brisco out as the perp. So, an arrest warrant for him was drafted by their PD and their patrol units have been on the lookout for him."

"What about the van?" asked Presler. "Any leads from those other prints?"

"There was blood found on the wheel and steering column, which suggest one of your bullets hit him. Where and how serious the injury to him is, we don't know. So, all the medical facilities in the area have been notified, just in case he shows up. I told you about AFIS matching up a print with an ex-con named Jim Ramirez, Sanchez and Cabrero apparently saw Ramirez and Brisco several times together in that van at a strip club in Maimi; a Cuban club called Amantes Latinas. They have surveillance photos of Ramirez that match up with his prior arrest photos. Search records show that Ramirez has a house in Sarasota. Sanchez is working on a search warrant for that location. Maybe Brisco's there. If not, who knows what we might find that would lead to him?"

10:16 AM
Orlando, Florida

Looking at the bandage around Brisco's right hand, Valverde asked, "Are you going to be able to drive?"

Before Brisco could respond, Valverde posed a deeper question, "What did happen to your hand?"

Brisco grinned. "I can drive. No problem." Holding up his injured hand, he added, "It's just from a little dust up I had with a guy."

"Of course. And I suspect that guy isn't doing too well right now." Then, throwing up his hands, Valverde said, "Forget I asked. I don't want to know the story behind it. Now, here, take the keys," Valverde said. "The wheels are around back."

"Where'd you get it?" asked Brisco.

"From a customer of mine. One of the businesses he owns is a used-car lot. He threw on some Michigan plates to throw off any cop looking for Jersey or Florida plates. The original owner was in an accident. My guy told him the car was totaled. It wasn't. The original owner signed over the title to him. The car was repaired and placed on the lot. Now you got it. When you get to Jersey, call me and one of my guys will make arrangement to have it picked up."

"What's in it for this car dealer of yours?" asked Brisco.

"Girls. He's a sex addict. He'll do what I ask, in exchange for some young escorts."

"And what's in it for you?"

"Three grand, and I get you out of here."

"What?! Are you kiddin' me? That's a lot of cash for a hot gun and temporary set of wheels."

"You got a better deal? Try Hertz."

"Man, you got me over a barrel. Give me a break. You know I'm good for the cash. Say two bills?"

"Twenty-five hundred; five for the gun, two for the car."

"All right, you're killing me. Looks like I've got no choice."

"Well?"

"Okay, okay; deal. One problem, though. I'll make good on the money. Don't worry about that. I just don't have any access to cash right now."

"I'm not worried. You might not have ready cash, but I'm sure your buddy Snake does."

"How would you know that?"

"I'm not stupid. The guy's a drug dealer. Granted, he might be a user, too. But from what I hear he can raise a lot of money fast, if he doesn't already have some of it stashed away somewhere. I want two bills by the end of the week. The other five by the first of the month. I don't care where it comes from. Rob a bank if you have to. Threaten Snake if you have to. I don't care how you do it or who you do it to, but I want my money. Got it?"

Brisco said, "I can call him and have him send you the two-and-a-half large. But I gotta have the gun, a box of ammo, and some cash for the trip."

"Okay, I can do that. I'll give you five hundred right now. I'll have a gun and a box of ammo put under the driver's seat, and then you have Snake send me three bills; the twenty-five and the five in cash I'll give you now. I'll even give you a break on that. No interest on the loan for the week. If the full three grand is not paid up in full by the end of next week, though, tack on another three-hundred to the bill."

Brisco shook his head. "The five hundred right now I get, but twenty-five hundred for a stolen gun, a box of ammo, and a several-day rental car. And a ten-percent vig. Man, you got some cojones. Okay, give me the five hundred now."

Valverde pulled out a wad of cash from his pocket and counted out five hundred dollars in fifties and twenties. Here you go. Don't spend it all in one place."

"Not funny," said Brisco as he pocketed the cash.

11:00 AM
Venice Police Department, Florida
and
Lavalette, New Jersey

"Hey, Cher, it's me."

"Everything okay down there, Mac? Are you okay?"

"Everything's fine. How are you and Hope doing? Enjoying the beach and boardwalk?"

"We've been having a good time with Ann and her kids. Jason has been acting his usual self . . . checking out everyone and everything, wherever we go."

"Good," said Mac. "I told him to keep a close eye on everyone."

"We'll be heading back north tomorrow," she said. "Will I see you then?"

"Yeah, I've arranged for an afternoon flight tomorrow into Newark. Marty will be staying down here."

"How'd you make out with that guy you two were looking for?"

"Still active."

Cheryl didn't like how that sounded. She knew her husband didn't care much for unfinished business. "What does that mean?" she asked.

"It means the local police and the Feds will be following up on this case down here. They've got some good leads to work on. Marty will make sure of that. We don't know where this guy will hit next—he's on the run—so, I'm heading back to make sure he doesn't pop up again in Jersey. He's running out of places to hide."

"Please be careful, Mac."

"I will, I will. I have a couple of calls I've got to make once I get back to the house. I hope to hit paydirt with one of them. I'll see you tomorrow, Cher. Tell Hope I'll give her a big hug when I get home. And tell your brother, I appreciate him looking out for all of you while I'm down here. I love you."

11:07 AM
Orlando, Florida

Brisco, Valverde, and Valverde's muscle went out the back door.

Looking at the red, 2011, Chevy sedan, Brisco said, "Red? That's the best you can do. Red stands out like a sore thumb."

"You get what you get, Bull," said Valverde. "The gun is under the front seat, loaded with two other mags, and a box of ammo in the glove box."

"Well, thanks for that. Untraceable?"

"A hot .38. Yeah, untraceable if you need to off it somewhere. You don't think for a minute my name or prints would be attached to it."

"The thought never entered my mind," said Brisco with a fading smile.

Before Brisco was about to get into the car, Valverde put his hand on the drug-addled, ex-con's shoulder. "And don't forget to make arrangements for Snake to pay me my three bills," he said.

"Is that it?" Brisco replied as he got in the vehicle.

"That's it. Now enjoy the trip!"

2:45 PM
Sarasota, Florida

Jimmy "the Snake" Ramirez was in his basement lifting weights when he thought he heard a knock on the front door. He then definitely heard a crash, followed by people yelling, "Police! Police!" He quickly ran upstairs. He only made it to the living room before he was met by several police officers.

"Police! Get down!" hollered one officer with his handgun extended and aimed directly at him. Ramirez put his hands in the air, went to his knees, then laid forward on the floor. He was cuffed and placed on a chair in the corner of the living room.

"You have a warrant?" the ex-con asked calmly.

"Right here," said Sanchez, placing a copy by Ramirez's feet as the other officers spread out searching the rest of the house for other occupants. Sanchez then read him his Constitutional Rights.

Ramirez was paying little attention to what Sanchez was saying.

He'd been read his Rights many times over the course of his criminal career. He knew to shut his mouth and ask for an attorney.

Looking down at the search warrant at his feet, Ramirez couldn't help but ask, "What's this for?"

"You can read it at your convenience, but basically, it's an anticipatory search warrant for your house and a copy of an arrest warrant for your buddy Alex Brisco. You both shared time in Trenton State. He's down here causing grief in Venice. You're here in Sarasota. Your prints were in his abandoned vehicle. Witnesses have seen you two together. We believe he's been staying here with you. In which case, you've been harboring a felon, and we anticipate—even if we don't find him here—we will find evidence of his presence. And anything else found while looking for that evidence is fair game. I'm talking about illegal drugs, guns, or other forms of contraband. That's the reason for this search warrant. It's all in there.

"Now, if we find nothing here, the cuffs come off and we leave. But if Brisco's here in your house, you will be charged with aiding and abetting a fugitive from justice. Short of that, if we just find *some* evidence of Brisco being here . . . like fingerprints, DNA, photos, address books . . . and any documents connecting you two to illicit activity — we still might be walking you down to police headquarters. Your prior convictions would be a slam dunk for aggravated circumstances at sentencing, if found guilty of new charges. That would put you right back in prison."

"Save your breath. I ain't talkin'. And I want an attorney."

"Hang tough, big boy," said Sanchez. "You're not under arrest right now."

"Then why am I cuffed?"

"To protect my guys and to prevent you from interfering with our investigation."

Sanchez then assigned an officer to stand guard over Ramirez as he decided to see how the search was going.

"Over here," said a DEA agent assigned to assist in the search. Wearing plastic gloves, he pointed to several used syringes laid out on the bench. "I found these in the garbage there with several empty vials. They were photographed along with the large number of full vials—they look like Deca bottles—and boxes of syringes over there in the corner."

"I'm a trafficking guy," said Sanchez, "not a drug guy. What's Deca?"

"Deca Durabolin, also known as Decabolin, or simply Durabolin," said the agent. "It's an anabolic steroid. Generic name Nandrolone Decanoate. There's another form of this stuff. Generic name Nandrolone Phenylpropionate. It's all basically the same shit. Comes only in liquid form. Powerful stuff. It's injected directly into muscle. Deca-Dura does have some legit medical use, but like all anabolic steroids it's mostly used by bodybuilders for muscle growth and strength. Other athletes have been known to use them for performance enhancement. Some bad side effects, though. One being the level of aggressiveness that comes with its use, which, at times, borders on rage. Be careful with these players, Carlos. Ramirez and company can go off on you any time, for any reason. And they have the strength of a bear."

"Thanks for the warning. He's cuffed and guarded in the living room right now." Sanchez looked at the large quantity of the suspected drugs in the corner of the basement and asked, "I take it this stash is highly illegal?"

"Under both federal and Florida law, it's illegal to sell, possess, or use these drugs. They're a schedule three narcotic. According to Florida law, an individual possessing an anabolic steroid can be charged with a third-degree felony which carries a maximum of a five-year prison sentence."

"All right, log 'em and have 'em sent to the lab. That's at least one charge we have so far against Ramirez. Good leverage for when he gets his attorney. A little cooperation might just shorten his prison sentence upon conviction."

Sanchez then headed upstairs. In one bedroom, an agent found two handguns, a rifle, and a combat knife. In the closet was a three-foot-tall metal filing cabinet filled with cash; mostly fifties, twenties, and tens.

"The weapons have all been, tagged, bagged, and ready to be sent to the lab," said the agent. "I'll run a serial number check on them when I get back to the office. Knowing this bunch, I'm sure they're either stolen or no record found on them."

"It'd be nice if they're found operable, with Brisco's prints on either of them, and if ballasts can connect a shooting to them. Just something else we can squeeze out of Ramirez if he decides to cooperate."

"As for the knife," Sanchez continued, "make sure you submit it for trace evidence. A speck of blood could be a homerun for us if we can get a DNA match with one of Ramirez's or Brisco's victims."

"And the cash?"

"Count it, log it, and wrap it. Have it sent to the field office." Sanchez then said, "Judging from all the drugs found in the basement, it looks like our guy here has been involved in distribution. That's another checkmark against our ex-con buddy in the other room."

Once the search was completed, Sanchez and the team perp-walked Ramirez to the marked patrol unit waiting for him by the curb.

13

AUGUST 16, 2015

3:30 AM
RICHMOND, VIRGINIA

The phone rang twelve times before Dillon Campo hit the call button.

"Hey, Ripper. Answer the damn phone!"

"Bull, is that you?"

"Yeah, it's me."

"Why you calling me at this hour? You woke my girl up. She's not very happy 'bout that."

"Too bad for her. I got some more news that ain't gonna make her feel any happier."

Campo was still half asleep from a long night of sex and drugs. "What are you talkin' about?"

"I'm going to be in Jersey soon. I should be up by Newark in three or four hours. I need a place to stay. I'm heading to your girl's place."

"Bull, I don't know if that's such a good idea. You're right, Marlene ain't gonna be happy 'bout that."

"Too freakin' bad. I got no choice. Things did not go well down here. The cops are looking for me. They got my van and a shotgun I left in it. I borrowed a car and some cash. I need to lay low for a day or two, 'til things blow over. I just need a place to crash for the time being."

"Okay, my brother. She'll just have to deal with it. Marlene's problem is she didn't like us shooting up in the house all the time. She thought you were a bad influence on me. Still does." Both ex-cons laughed.

"That's rich, Dillon," said Brisco, "considering you were my drug source. I guess she doesn't know that part of the story."

"And I like to keep it that way."

"Hey, have you heard from Snake at all?" asked Brisco.

"No, why, was I supposed to?"

"I called him several times. No answer. I owe Valverde money. I need Snake to take care of that for me."

"You'll be here soon. Call him again later today."

"I just got a bad feeling about this. Cops are swarming all over the place looking for me down there. Hopefully, they haven't focused in on him."

"Don't worry. If they did, he'd keep his mouth shut."

"Yeah, that's not my worry. Valverde will want his money. No tellin' what he'd do."

"We can sort that all out when you get here."

"All right. Well, I'm starting to fade. I'll pop another pill and see you in a few more hours. We're talkin' the same place . . . the one on Pulaski in the North Ironbound section?"

"Yep, same place, the three-story walkup where you stayed with us for two weeks last month . . . when you were here on business."

3:53 AM
Orlando, Florida

Maria Consuelo Alvarez Rodriguez was naked, tied spread eagled to the bedposts, and a strip of duct tape was over her mouth. Two of

Valverde's men stood over her waiting for a signal from their boss.

Jill Morgan and Maureen Sorbo sat in the corner of the room alongside Maglia Selina.

Valverde walked in. "Okay, girls, babysitting time is over," he said. "I've run out of patience. Here's the deal. You on the bed will be raped repeatedly by my guys here. Then you will be beaten, given a hot load of heroin, and dumped way out in the ocean to be breakfast for the fish. Cost of doing business."

Maria squirmed about on the bed, tears flowing down her face.

"Oh, my God!" cried Jill.

"Why are you doing this, you animal?!" said Maureen as she reached over and put her arm around Jill.

"Because I can," said Valverde. He then added, "There's one way, however, that that whole situation can be avoided."

Maria's eyes widened, as did Jill's and Maureen's.

"Simply put, I need you girls to cooperate. If you do, you two can save this girl's life. That's a good deed, right?"

"What do you want us to do?" asked Maureen.

"Well, for starters, you're going to take on new names." Looking at Jill, he said, "Your new name from now on is Candy. And you, Miss Curiosity, will be called Cat. This one on the bed I think the name Mona would be fitting. But Mora would be a more marketable name . . . so Mora it is.

"Secondly, Candy, you will go with Maggie after the sun comes up. She will get you up to speed on waiting tables. This is a strip club so you will be topless. For Mora's sake, can you handle that?"

Jill put her head down and nodded.

"I need a smile."

Jill lifted her head and forced an expression that looked more like a smirk.

"Good, but we can do better. Let's try it again. And remember, Mora's life depends on it."

Jill took a deep breath and smiled.

"Much, much better. You'll do fine at the bar. A lot of tips should come your way."

Valverde then looked at Maureen. "Now, you, Cat, will go with my guys across town. I have a Cuban escort service there. You'll fit right in. I have faith you'll cooperate fully and with joy. If you don't, there are many ways you or one of these girls will pay a deadly price."

Pointing to Maria on the bed, Maureen asked, "What about her?"

"Mora will be fine. She'll either join Candy at the bar—or else,—what's the old Mafia saying, 'she'll swim with the fish.'"

Valverde then clapped his hands. "That's it, ladies. Now get some rest." Just before walking out of the room, he turned, and with a broad grin, said, "Your Cinderella moments await you."

4:15 PM
Newark/Lyndhurst, New Jersey

"Hey, Jason, it's me, Mac. I just landed. I should be home in about 30 minutes."

"Yo, bro. Why didn't you call me for a ride?!"

"Best you stay with the girls. I'll catch a ride here."

"Well, good to have you back."

"Good to be back. I spoke with Cheryl yesterday. She said they had a good time at your shore house. Thanks for keeping an eye on them."

"Yeah, it was quiet down there. No surprises. Cheryl told me you didn't get the guy you were looking for, that Brisco guy. What's going on with that?

"There's a lot of people looking for him right now; Venice PD, Miami PD, and ICE, to name just a few. When I get back to my office, I have to make a call to Bergen County Detective Arnet and update him on what happened down in Venice."

"And what was that?"

"Marty Presler and I had a brief encounter with our boy. He shot up Marty's car and we shot up his. Unfortunately, he got away, thanks to two ICE guys who stopped us from pursuing him."

"Why'd they do that?"

"Long story. Here's the short of it: apparently, they were surveilling Brisco and when the shooting started, they didn't know what was going on. Seems they figured they could always find him, but since they hadn't a clue who we were or why we were shooting at him, they stopped us. The good news, though, is that no charges were lodged against Marty or me for an unlawful use of weapons, discharging weapons in public, or any other charge the local DA might have wanted to tack on. I do like that 'stand your ground' legislation that they have down there."

"Well, that's good news. What's the story with Brisco now? Do you think he's still down there, or is he on the run?"

"Hard to tell. The Feds and plenty of locals are looking for him. They'll be turning over a lot of rocks. If I were him, I'd be heading out of town as fast as I could."

"So that's why you headed back so soon. You think he might be heading back up this way."

"Could be, Jason. This guy has killed two people up here. He grew up in Jersey. He's got connections here. There's a comfort level for many of these guys when it comes to hiding out. Familiar surroundings make it easier for them to blend in. At least in their minds it does. For us, though, it provides a wealth of leads: friends, houses, places of business, places to hang out, family. Which reminds me, I have another call to make when I get back to the office."

"Who's that?"

"He's a hacker. He might have a lead or two on Brisco's whereabouts."

"Good luck with that. In the meantime, Cheryl and Hope will be at my house until you get home. Then I could drop them off."

"No, no. Change of plan. Listen, have them stay with you a bit longer. I don't know what this nut case is up to, but I suspect he'll visit here first. I don't want Cheryl and Hope here in case he does show up. I don't know what he knows and what he doesn't know. I have no idea what's on his radar screen. It's just a gut feeling, but I think if I were in his shoes, I'd still make my place target one."

"Okay, Mac. I've had the locals on board here, running routine pass-bys. In the event Brisco has a different plan of attack, we should be okay here. Just keep me in the loop."

"Thanks, Jay. I will. See you soon."

6:27 PM
ORLANDO, FLORIDA
AND
NEWARK, NEW JERSEY

"Where's my money, Bull?! I called Snake several times since you left. No answer."

"Benito, I've reached out to Snake, too, several times yesterday afternoon and all day today. Nothing. Nada. No answer. I don't like it."

"You don't like it? You owe me three bills! I'm not a patient man. If you can't get it from him, get it from someone else. Just get it!"

"You know where I'm at right now. If I get my hands on the money here, how will I get it to you?"

"Let me worry about that. Just let me know when you have it. As for your buddy Snake, I'll have my guys check the house and see what that's all about. If he's there, they'll get the money. If he's not there, they might have to break in. If that's the case, let me know where the cash is kept."

"Benito, if I let you know where the cash is, I'd never see a penny left in the box. Here's a better plan. If I can get the cash up here, I can give it to whoever is going to pick up the car."

"Okay. Good to know, though, that your cash is in a box somewhere in the house."

Brisco was feeling a white heat building up inside him. "Keep your guys out of Snake's house! I'll get you your money! If I don't hear back from him soon, I'll get the cash I owe you in a few days from someplace else. You told me I had a week; a little longer with interest if I had a problem raising it."

"That's when I knew Snake was reachable. I haven't heard from him since you left. So, the deal has changed. You've got two days to come up with the cash."

14

AUGUST 17, 2015

9:30 AM
SARASOTA COUNTY JAIL, FLORIDA

Sanchez and Cabrero sat on one side of the metal conference table. Jimmy Ramirez and his attorney, Public Defender Paul Dresen, sat on the other side. "So, you have some information you want to share with us," Cabrero said as Sanchez prepared to take notes of the interview.

Dresen put his hand across Ramirez's chest just as the arrestee was going to answer. Dresen then said, "I spoke with the deputy attorney general on this case. He said he'd be willing to consider dropping or downgrading some charges or offering immunity to my client for any statement he gives to you, depending on how good the information is. He wants to hear it, first. Right now, I explained to my client that should he be convicted of the false charges lodged against him, he'll go away for a long, long time. He understands that. He also understands that if he fully cooperates, he would be in a very dangerous position, both in jail and out. So, I need your assurance that once we're finished here, he won't be put back in the general population. Ideally, we can get his bail reduced and he can get out of here."

"You know we have a strong case against him. You call them

'false charges.' I don't think you'd like to defend against those charges in court. I guess that's why you're here. If your client has good information, solid information, then whatever deal the DAG offered you is on the table."

Cabrero directed his stare at Ramirez, "So, Jimmy, why don't you start by telling us the story behind the drugs, guns, and money found in your house."

Ramirez looked at Dresen. Dresen nodded.

"Look, I know what you guys want from me. I'm not a snitch. But I ain't goin' back to prison for the rest of my life because of Bull."

"Bull?"

"Bull, Briz, Brisco. I think his first name is Alex, but nobody calls him that."

"Okay," said Cabrero, "we'll get to him. Right now, get back to the drugs, guns, and money."

"Look, I admit, I'm on the juice. I work out in my basement whenever I can. I'm just a user."

Cabrero looked at Dresen. "Is this how this is going to go?"

Dresen put his arm on Ramirez's shoulder. "Tell them what you told me."

"Yeah, well, okay. Bull and I sell the shit, as well as use it."

"Where do you get it?"

"Some guy in Miami."

"Some guy? Who is he?"

"Man, you guys are going to put me in a bad place."

"Not to worry. We'll use it as intelligence until we can get something actionable that could corroborate what you're telling us. Go on . . . what's his name?"

"Valverde, Benito Valverde. He owns a strip club in Miami named Latinas and another club in Orlando. I don't remember the name."

Both Cabrero and Sanchez remained poker-faced.

"And the guns? Same guy?"

"Well, yeah. He's got connections all over."

"How about women . . . girls?" asked Cabrero.

"What about 'em?"

"Where does he get the girls for the club? If he's into drugs and guns, I suspect he's into trafficking women, too."

Ramirez looked again at Dresen. "Go ahead, answer the question."

"I don't know where he gets the girls. I guess some are druggies; runaways; some from broken homes; some just like to dance, or like being naked. I don't know."

"How about those smuggled into the country and put to work? You know anything about that?"

"Maybe."

"What do you mean maybe?"

"I know Bull and him had talked about bringing girls from his club in Miami to the one over in Orlando. It's a Cuban neighborhood. Maybe the girls are illegal Cubans."

"What's the name of his club in Orlando?"

"It's a Spanish name for girls . . . I think."

Cabrero said, "Chicas."

"Yeah, yeah. That's it. Chicas."

"And the one in Miami. What's the name of that club?"

"Latinas"

"Amantes Latinas."

"Yup. You got it. Latin Lovers. You know the place?"

Cabrero ignored the question. "You said Bull and Valverde talked about bringing girls from Miami to Orlando. What do you know about that?"

"Only that some of the mangos might be young. That they might be underaged, or illegal. Bull didn't seem to care. As long as he got paid, Valverde could ask him to do anything . . . and he'd do it . . . for a buck.

"Did he ever tell you about killing anyone?"

"Not directly."

"How about indirectly?"

"We'll yeah. He talked about some girl and some guy up in Jersey who he took care of."

"Took care of?"

"I guess he meant kill them . . . but he didn't say that," said Ramirez.

"How about two Newark detectives. Did he say anything about them?"

"Yeah, he said he had a score to settle with them."

"Names? Who are they?"

"Some guys named Taylor and Presler."

"You seem to know quite a bit about his vendettas," said Cabrero.

"Just what he told me. I don't know anything else."

"All right. How'd you meet him?"

"I met Bull in Trenton State. I got out a lot earlier than him. When he got out, he looked me up. He wanted to get back in the game, so recently I introduced him to Valverde. Valverde took a liking to him and planned to have more work for him. He wanted to keep him busy, but Bull gets a little crazy at times. Sometimes, he just ups and disappears. Not sure if Valverde is okay with that."

"You said 'keep him busy'. . . how would Valverde keep him busy?" asked Cabrero.

"He was more an enforcer-type guy, more than just routine muscle. I think Valverde liked that about him. He wasn't called Bull for nothing. If you knew him, you knew never to cross him. If he knew I was talking to you guys, I'd be dead in a week. No con likes a rat. And Bull is a con on steroids. Literally! So, you gotta make sure he doesn't find out."

"Will do, Jimmy. I can call you Jimmy, right?"

"Sure, why not? It's my name."

"You also go by the name Snake, right?"

"Yeah."

"What do you prefer to be called."

"My friends call me Snake. You can call me Jimmy."

"Okay, *Jimmy*. Now Carlos and I will protect your interests, make sure you're safe. In exchange, we want to know everything you know about Bull."

It was Dresen who spoke this time. "Does that mean you'll speak with the DAG about dropping charges, amending charges, lowering bail, or offering some form of immunity for my client?"

"If he tells us all he knows about Brisco and this guy Valverde. And he does one other thing for us. Then yeah. We have a deal."

9:53 AM
Newark, New Jersey

"I want him out of here, Dillon!" said Marlene Rivera. "He nothing but trouble. And he's gonna get you in trouble. I know it. I can feel it."

"He's my bud," replied Campo. "I can't ask him to leave. I won't. We're business partners. He's here on business . . . and he's just staying a short time. Only a couple of days, I suspect."

"Why are you partners with him? He scares the shit outta me."

"Relax, babe. I'm here. You don't need to worry 'bout him. Besides, like I said, he'll be gone in a couple of days."

Brisco sat on the living room couch and swallowed down some pills just as Campo entered the room. He then took out a syringe and a vial of Decabolin.

"Still stackin' I see," said Campo. "I don't have any iron here, though, for you to burn up some energy."

"I'll be okay after a few hundred down reps." Brisco got up and walked to the window. He looked down on the street, then began to pace the room.

"You okay?" asked Campo.

"We need to talk, Ripper."

"If it's about those locations you asked me to check out, there was nothing I could do. Nobody was at either place."

"That's not it. I need cash, three grand actually, and I need wheels. I keep calling Snake but he never answers his phone. I got money at his house but no way to get at it. And some guy will be picking up my car outside sometime today or tomorrow. It was part of a deal I had with Valverde. Who, by the way, is who I owe the money to."

"I wish I could help you, but I don't have that kind of money with me. You can borrow my car, though, if you need something to get around."

"What about your girl? Can she get her hands on the cash?"

"I don't want to bring her into this, Bull. She don't like you being here as it is. I told her you're only going to be here a few days. No way she's gonna give you money."

"I ain't asking, Ripper. If she's got the money, I need it. I don't need Valverde's goons breathing down my neck, especially now that I have a score to settle with a guy named Taylor."

"I don't know."

"Tell her it's money you owe a bookie, or drug dealer, or loan shark. Tell her he's going to break some bones if he doesn't get the money. She doesn't want to see anything happen to you, right? You can tell her you'll pay her back."

"Yeah, like that's ever gonna happen. I know you, Bull. Once you get your hands on the cash, it's gone. Then I'm stuck with a three-thousand-dollar bill, which, of course, I'm never going to pay. End of relationship."

"Just tell her to get the money, or else."

"Or else, what?!"

Brisco gave Campo a hard look. "Ripper, you really don't want to know that answer. We are partners, she ain't. You might like her, but she means nothing to me. I need the money. She has it, I want it." He then turned from Campo, dropped down on the floor, and began pumping out alternate one-arm push-ups.

15
AUGUST 18, 2015

12:10 PM
SARASOTA COUNTY JAIL, FLORIDA

"Just for the record, I'm not liking this other thing you want from my client." Dresen asked.

"It's a simple thing, counselor. We just want him to make a phone call. That's all. No big deal," said Cabrero. "We searched your client's cell phone and came up with Brisco's number on speed dial. We need to know where Brisco is now and what he's up to."

"I can answer both questions without calling him," said Ramirez. "He should be in Jersey right now at Campo's girlfriend's place."

"Who are they?"

"Ripper and his girlfriend."

"Who?"

"His name is Dillon Campo. We call him Ripper."

"We?"

"Briz, me, Valverde. Not sure how he got that handle. I suspect he got it in prison 'cause he liked to cut people like that English guy, Jack the Ripper. I think I heard that from some guy he did time with. As for his girl, she lives somewhere in Newark. I haven't been there or heard him talking about where in Jersey it is, but that's where Bull was headed. I guess he went there for two reasons. One, there was too much heat on him down here after that Venice fiasco; and two, he's got a score to settle up there."

"That score being Taylor?"

"I guess."

"What's his girlfriend's name?"

"I don't know."

"We need to know where she lives, so we want you to make the call anyway. We might be able to zero in on his location that way."

"Then he'll know I set him up. I'm dead meat then."

"He won't know how we located him. We'll have that covered. Even if he figures your phone or his was being traced, he wouldn't know it was intentional on your part. Right now, we have several missed calls made by him on your phone. He'll wonder why you didn't call him back. When he asks, and he will ask, tell him you lost your phone. You looked for it all over and couldn't find it. You eventually went to the phone company and got a new one. They were able to give you a new phone with the same number. Okay?"

"I don't know if he'll buy it."

"Sure, he will," said Sanchez.

"I'm not advising Dillon to do a consensual overhear," said Dresen. "That's too risky."

"Maybe so, counselor," said Cabrero, "but that's the deal we're offering. Besides, anything that spins off of the conversation will be kept off the record. That I can promise you."

"All due respect, Agent Cabrero, promises by the police mean nothing. I don't trust you; you don't trust me. I have to do what's best for my client, and this deal only hurts him."

"Are you kidding me?!" Sanchez laughed aloud when he heard that. "Your boy here gets to walk from several, very serious charges; charges that would put him away for a very long time; effectively, his whole life, if you want to call it a life. This way, he helps us, we help him. Brisco's going away for a long time once he's caught. And eventually he will be caught. We just want to shorten the search for him before he causes any more damage. With Jimmy's help here, we can accomplish that. In return, he gets his Brownie points and skates jail. There won't be anything in court records other than a C.I. number to attach Jimmy here to Brisco. And as you know, confidential informants aren't unmasked except in some very unusual circumstances, and this isn't one of them. So, it's your call. Remember, we get paid whether he cooperates or not. We've got nothing on the line. He's got his whole life on the line. Your call."

"All right, Jimmy, it's your decision," said Dresen. "I'm not recommending doing it, but it's not me who's facing 30 plus years in jail."

"Okay," said Ramirez. "I'm not going back in the can, if I can help it. I'll do it. I won't push him, though. I don't want him too suspicious of what's going on."

"Terrific. Let's sign you out, take you to our office, and dial him up. Are you ready for a three-and-a-half-hour trip to Miami?"

"Anything to get the hell outta here," said Ramirez.

"Okay with you, counselor?"

"Take good care of him. I won't be joining you. I'll call your DAG, though, about getting his bail and charges dropped or reduced, with no jail time, because of his cooperation as a confidential informant."

"Sounds like a plan," said Cabrero. "We're on board with that."

Cabrero then called his tech people in Miami to set up for a consensual overhear and to get the telephone company to prepare to triangulate cell towers on Brisco's cell phone.

1:14 PM
Venice, Florida
and
Bloomfield, New Jersey

"Hi, Mac, McDaniel here."

"Hey, Sarge. What's up?"

"Just got some information from Agent Cabrero that he wants to have passed on to you. He's interviewing a guy who said Brisco's heading north. He's suspected of staying somewhere in Newark; at the house or apartment of a girlfriend of Dillon Campo, aka Ripper. No further information at this time, but Cabrero's working on it. We have an APB on an arrest warrant we put out on Brisco. I suspect he'll be looking for you. So, be prepared for a visit from him unless he's picked up before he reaches you. Cabrero and Sanchez have some work left to do with Brisco's pal. Then they'll be heading to Miami on another lead this guy gave them."

"Who's the guy giving them all this info?"

"They arrested a guy who's now a C.I. They won't give up the name, but Cabrero did say they busted him for guns, drugs, and drug money. Brisco lived with him on and off. He's looking at some serious time, so he's desperate to make a deal. So far, he told Sanchez and Cabrero that after that altercation with you and your buddy, Brisco told him he needed to get out of town. He's pretty confident Brisco's heading up your way to where Campo is."

"Did you get anything on a vehicle he might be driving?"

"No. The C.I. only suspects he'll be driving north. Nothing to substantiate that. Just giving you a heads up as a precaution."

"I appreciate that. You said Sanchez and Cabrero are going to Miami. If Brisco's heading north, why are they heading south? What's that all about?"

"Those guys are with the human-trafficking section of ICE.

Ramirez gave them a lead on a strip club in Miami where sex-trafficking might be taking place. That's their first order of business. They want Brisco, but he'll have to wait. They want a big fish, too; a guy named Benito Valverde who owns the strip club Amantes Latinas in Miami, as well as a club in Orlando . . . and who they suspect is, in fact, trafficking women, drugs, and young girls."

"Well, thanks for the info, Sarge. I hope they get this guy Valverde. In the meantime, I'll keep a sharp eye out for my dirtbag avenger. I'll let you know if I learn anything."

5:07 PM
Immigration and Customs Enforcement (ICE) Field Office
Miami, Florida
and
Newark, New Jersey

Sanchez pulled his assigned undercover car into the back entrance of the building.

Cabrero sat in the front passenger seat. Detective Sergeant McDaniel sat next to Ramirez in the back seat. Ramirez was wearing the standard prisoner transport handcuffs: a leather belt connected in the back with a metal ring in front. A set of handcuffs attached to the metal ring.

"Can you finally take these cuffs off?" said Ramirez.

"Easy there. They'll come off once we get in a secured location inside," said Sanchez. "We don't want to see you do anything stupid, like try to run on us."

"Where the hell would I go?!"

"Well, we're not going to find out."

The four individuals were buzzed into the rear of the building after notification on the intercom. They were then let in through a metal gate that was unlocked by a security guard. Once inside,

McDaniel removed the handcuff and belt from Ramirez. They then entered a back windowless room that had a table and several chairs in it. On the table was a writing pad, a pen, pencil, and a recorder with headphones attached. A loose wire also hung from the recorder.

"Have a seat," said Sanchez to Ramirez.

The others also sat down around the table.

Technician Specialist Jack Harding walked into the room. "Carlos, we have the paperwork for the intercept. Let me know when you're ready."

"We're ready now, Jack."

Harding left the room.

Sanchez took out a plastic bag from his pocket that contained Ramirez's cell phone. He put on a pair of plastic gloves from his other pocket, took the phone out of the bag, and connected it to the loose wire. He handed the phone to Ramirez.

"Jimmy, you're going to call Brisco. The conversation will be recorded, and we'll hear everything that's being said. If he asks you why you didn't get back to him sooner, remember what we told you to say, 'You lost your phone.' Here's what we want to know: one, where he is; two, has he been in touch with Valverde; and three, anything he knows about girls going in and coming out of Valverde's strip clubs. It'd be a grand slam if he admits to any of his murders or spinoff crimes. But that might be a bit too much to ask. Don't push him, or he'll suspect something's up. I will write questions for you to ask him as we go along. Just relax and go with the flow. He won't suspect a thing."

"Yeah, right. He ain't stupid."

"Just be yourself with him. Okay?"

"All right."

Sanchez, Cabrero, and McDaniel put on the headphones. Sanchez then said, "Make the call."

Brisco's phone rang twice before he hit the call button.

"Bull, it's me."

"Where the hell have you been?! I've been calling you for the last couple of days!"

"It's been a nightmare, Bull. I had my phone with me the last time we were together but later in the day, I couldn't find it. I don't know where it could be. Still don't. I checked everywhere. Maybe it's in that room at Valverde's where we were, when I dropped you off. I hate having to go back there and see him again."

"Something ain't right. You just called me on your number."

Sanchez scribbled down some words and turned the pad toward Ramirez.

"Yeah, well, I went to the phone company a little while ago. They gave me a new phone and were able to program in my old number."

"Well, at least you're back on line now. Listen, you have to go back and see Valverde. I owe him three grand. Take the money from the house and bring it to him. He was going to send some of his goons to your house to look for the money. We can't let that happen. I'll call him and tell him you're on your way with the money."

Sanchez scribbled again and turned the pad.

"Bull, I'll call Valverde if you want and let him know I'll have the money for him."

"We'll both call him. I don't want any problems here. He did me a solid with the car and gun, but I still don't trust him. He might rat me out or put a hit out on me if he doesn't get his cash. He's a sleazebag."

"Yeah, I don't trust him at all, either."

"Glad you got my back. When you didn't answer the phone, I wanted Ripper and his girl to front me the money. They weren't going to do it. I wasn't liking that at all. I won't forget."

Sanchez scribbled and turned the pad.

"Ripper's been with us a long time. I hope you're not planning to put him and her on the list along with those other guys? He's been good for us. He's even given you a place to stay up there. Give him some slack, now that I can take care of this matter with Valverde."

"Okay. They're off the list . . . for now." Brisco laughed into the phone. "Just get back to me when you square up with that cheap bastard Valverde."

Sanchez scribbled and held up the pad.

"Oh, before you go, Bull, if Valverde wants to move some mangos, are you in? When are you coming back?"

"I don't know when I'll be back. In the meantime, keep me informed on what Valverde's up to. The money is good, but he'll cut me out if I'm not around."

"Yeah, that last package we took to Orlando was easy money. The girls didn't give us an ounce of problems. And Valverde made good on the deal. There should be other deals like that coming up."

"I hear ya. . . . Okay, gotta go. Don't forget. Take care of that situation with him. I don't need his monkeys out lookin' for me, too. I've got enough problems with the cops on my ass."

"Okay, Briz. I'll be in touch," said Ramirez.

"You'd better," replied Brisco.

The call ended.

Jack Harding entered the room. "He had to be calling from a car. His location kept moving. We had him on various streets in Newark. Our last location on him, though, was on Bloomfield Avenue in Bloomfield, New Jersey.

5:31 PM
Miami, Florida
and
Bloomfield, New Jersey

"Mac, it's me again," said Detective Sergeant McDaniel.

"Jack, what's up?"

"Just got some new info. Brisco is currently in Newark and Bloomfield. He's moving around, so he's in a vehicle of some sort."

"How'd you come by that?"

"Our guy here called him, and the telephone company was able to triangulate the cell towers he was using. A few minutes ago, he was on Bloomfield Avenue in your town. Can't think of any reason for him being there other than to meet up with you."

"Thanks, Jack. I figured it was only a matter of time with this psychopath. I'll be ready for him if he stops by. Anything on the vehicle he's in?"

"No, the conversation didn't head in that direction. Mostly about money, girls, and where he's been staying. They didn't want to get too deep. They thought that might spook him. He's staying in Newark, though, with those two I told you about; that guy Campo and his girlfriend. We don't have her name, so we don't know where she lives in Newark. If and when we get something on that, I'll let you know."

"Sounds good. Thanks again for the heads up. Let's talk again. Right now, I have to get ready for a 'surprise visit.'"

"Good luck."

5:37 PM
Bloomfield, New Jersey

Mac slowly opened the lower desk drawer in his office. He took out his .40 and .45 Glock handguns, along with two holsters. He quietly loaded the handguns, put the .40 in his shoulder holster and the forty-five in his waistband holster. He then, closed the desk drawer ever so slowly. He stood silent for a minute, listening for any noise. Not hearing any, he removed the .45 and, holding it at a point-shoulder level, checked all the rooms in his house. Once he determined he was the only occupant there, he called Jason.

"They okay?" Mac asked.

"Yeah, the girls are fine. Why? You, okay?"

"No signs of him here . . . yet."

"Well, I'm a little ticked off you didn't want me to come with you."

"I told you I wanted you to keep an eye on the girls. This guy will get at me and Marty anyway he can."

"Okay, but that doesn't explain why you didn't call the locals down there to respond."

"Jason, this guy's got a death wish. I don't want to go to another brother officer's funeral, especially if it was on my account. Besides, I don't want this dirtbag arrested. I want to put this vendetta he has for me, Marty, and our families to rest. And there'll be no rest . . . until he's put to rest.

"Anyway, thanks again, my brother, for taking care of the girls. Now, if Cheryl is nearby, could you put her on the phone?"

Moments later Cheryl took the receiver from Jason's hand.

"Hello?"

"Hi, honey, I'm at the house. I'll be coming over to see you soon. It'd be best if you stay with Ann and Jason for the time being. I'll explain it all when I get there."

"Why? Is he here, the guy after you?!" Cherly asked.

"Reports are he's in Bloomfield as we speak, so I don't want to take any chances that he's checking out our house."

"I'm so tired of this, Mac. You don't know."

"I know, honey. I wish things were different, but they're not. It's the hand we're dealt."

"It's the hand you're dealt! Hope and I just happen to be potential collateral damage."

"I know. I'm sorry you and Hope are caught up in all this. We can talk when I get there. You know I love both of you, and I don't want anything bad to happen to either of you."

"I know. And I love you, too. But this can't keep going on. My brother and Ann are great, but I need to be in my own home. I miss my home."

"I know. Hopefully, this will all be over soon."

"Yes, hopefully. I'll see you when I'll see you," Cheryl said matter-of-factly, before hanging up.

After the call ended, Mac sat, wondering if the life he chose as a soldier, a cop, and a private investigator was worth it all. Was it fair to the people he loved. Putting them in danger because of the unsavory elements he brought into his life and, in effect, theirs. He knew he couldn't turn off the spicket. The fight was in his blood. But was it fair to them? He thought long and hard about the life he chose, living on the edge, and how it affected his loved ones. It wasn't fair to them. Mac knew that. Getting up from his desk, he walked into the kitchen and, after pouring himself a stiff Scotch and water, headed upstairs to relax. Finishing off the drink, it was then he made a final solemn oath: *the chaos needed to end—for good—and to end soon.*

Meanwhile, Brisco drove slowly down the street. He parked the sedan several houses down from Mac and Cheryl's place. He put the gun Valverde gave him in his right pocket. Approaching Taylor's house, he noticed the car and truck in the driveway. He ducked behind a bush to his right, then edged his way along the side of the house. Sneaking a glimpse into one of the windows and not seeing any activity, he continued to the rear of the house. Again, no activity seen through the rear windows. As he came around the other side of the building, Brisco saw the door that led to Mac's office. He was hoping to break in, catch Mac and family by surprise, and kill them all. If they were home during the day, any alarm system would be off. If not home, he wasn't sure he'd want to take the chance of breaking in. *Too much attention and not much, if anything, to accomplish there,* he thought.

So Brisco waited. He again peered into several windows. He did not hear or see any activity inside the house. Not true, though, for the neighborhood. Dog walkers, bicyclists, joggers, and routine motor-vehicle traffic presented somewhat of a problem for him. Brisco concluded, even though there was a car and truck in the driveway, no one was home at Mac's house and that a break-in might set off an alarm. Plus, with all the neighborhood activity, someone was bound to spot him. An eyewitness helped put him in jail for thirty years the last time. He did not want to chance that again. Reluctantly, Brisco decided to return to his car and try another time, another way, to take down Taylor. *Time now to make a phone call.*

16
AUGUST 19, 2015

8:02 AM
Sarasota/Miami, Florida

"Hey, Benito. It's me, Snake."

"I was waiting for your call. I spoke with Bull last night. He said he got in touch with you and you have my money."

"Yeah, no problem, I got it."

"Good, you can drop it off with Maggie at the club."

"See, here's the thing. I got the cash, and I can drop it off today. One problem, though. There's an undercover sitting on my place. They must know that Bull has been staying here. These mutts think I don't know they're there. Cops ain't so sharp as they'd like us to believe."

"What's the problem, then?"

"I don't want them to put a tail on me that will lead right to your place. Next thing you know they'll want to flip your joint. That would not be good. Wouldn't you agree?"

"Okay, so what's the deal. How do I get my money and keep the cops away?"

"I've been supplying dope to a guy who comes from a very rich family. I'll give him a call and tell him to front me the cash. I'll tell him to bring the money to you . . . that I can't bring the money 'cause I'm in bed here with a high fever."

"And why would this 'guy from a rich family' do this for you?"

"I'll tell him he'll get a free ride until the three-grand mark is reached. He'll do it, or I'll tell him the well is dry. This kid loves his dope. Besides, he trusts me. That's funny, Benito. Ain't it? We don't trust anybody. This kid will learn in time."

"Well, you're asking me to trust you with this guy; a guy I know nothing about. Don't play with me."

"I swear on my life, this guy is legit."

"And if he's not, I'm going to take you up on that."

"He's good, Benito. Believe me. I wouldn't lie to you. I know what the consequences are."

"You better be square with me on this. He comes alone got that?"

"Okay, okay. I got it."

"What's his name? What's he look like?"

"His name is Emanuel Hernández. He likes to be called Manny. He's Spanish, maybe Cuban. Average height, maybe five-seven."

"You say he's got money. What's the family business?"

"Some financial bullshit. I'm not sure. I heard him mention once that his dad handles pension investments; for who, what, and where, I don't know. But there's big money in those pensions. The kid does business out of Orlando, so he could meet you at Chicas."

"Okay, send him over. I'll be there later on today. He might be someone I can work with in the future. Always looking for new opportunities to make money."

"I'll punch him a call then," Ramirez said before hitting the end button on his cell phone.

Cabrero disconnected the phone from the recorder.

Sanchez sat back in his chair. "You did well, Jimmy."

"Yeah, for you. Not me. I just have to make sure Valverde and Brisco don't find out I'm cooperating with you guys. If they do, I'm as good as dead. Now that's a fact."

"We'll do everything we can to protect you. You can cool your heels in one of our hideaways for the time being. Relax, we'll take it from here." Sanchez then turned to Cabrero and smiled. "It's been a while since I used my undercover name, Manny Hernández. Let's see how this goes."

9:15 AM
Verona/Newark, New Jersey

"Springer, how ya doin'? asked Brisco.

"Didn't you promise not to call me again?!"

"Yeah, I changed my mind. I need some more information."

"I can see this nightmare isn't going to end soon. What do you want now?"

"I need information on where Taylor shops, where he spends his time and money."

"I told you about his business, his friends and his associates. It's not easy hacking into his credit card. I've gotten into his email accounts, but for a credit-card lookup I need a lot of personal questions answered. This isn't like the movies. I don't just hit a few buttons and I'm in."

"Well, maybe his email accounts will give you something. Get back to me.

"Oh, and, by the way, I don't know how Presler or Taylor knew I was coming to the Venice pier, but I'll find out who tipped them off. You gave me the location, right, Springer? But you wouldn't have double-crossed me. It couldn't have been you, 'cause you know what would happen to you if you did. So, I'm giving you a chance to get that information on Taylor for me. If you don't or if Taylor has a heads up on the information I'm looking for, well then, I know what side of the fence you're on. And you know what that means."

9:27 AM
Verona/Bloomfield, New Jersey

"Hello, Mr. Taylor."

"Yeah, Springer, you have something for me?"

"I just got a call from Brisco. He knows! He knows I gave you the information about Venice. He's going to kill me. I know it!"

"Calm down, kid."

"I can't calm down! He threatened to kill me if I didn't give him more information on you. I suspect he'd kill me anyway, even if I did! The man is a psychopath! I wish I never heard of him or you!"

"You have to settle down. Look, call you lawyer. Maybe he can work out something with the police for protection. That's if he and you decide to go that route. After all, Brisco dragged you into this mess. You cooperated with him. To do what? To kill me! So don't blame me for your situation. I'll help you, how and when I can, but you have to do what I need you to do."

"I can't believe this is happening."

"Just lay low for a while. Does he know where you live?"

"I don't know. I don't think so."

"Good, if you have a friend you can stay with for a week or two, do it. I hope to take care of this Brisco within that time frame. He can't go on threatening to kill everyone he comes in contact with. Right now, I need to find a time and place to meet him so we can settle this score. So, what info does he want about me?"

"He wants additional information on where you spend your time and money. He wants credit card information on you. I told him I can get email info for him, but getting into your credit-card account might be too far a jump. I left it up in the air, though, that it's a possibility. I figure I'd let you decide how you wanted to handle that."

"Well, first off, I don't want you accessing any information from *any* of my accounts, which includes my email accounts. But it's good you called. Just let me think about the next move for a minute."

"Whatever you decide, he's going to suspect you're on to him. If you don't stop him on your next encounter, I'm dead meat. He's definitely going to kill me."

Mac wasn't paying attention to Springer's last comment. His mind was elsewhere.

"Here's what I want you to do," he said. "Give it an hour and call Brisco back. Say you couldn't get into my credit-card account, but you saw on my email that I'm meeting some guy named Jason for lunch tomorrow at Giglio's Italian Restaurant on Bloomfield Avenue. Tell him we're to meet at around 12:30."

"I guess I should write this down."

"Yeah, you don't want to screw this up. And do yourself a favor, don't give him any info that would lead him to believe you're plotting with me against him."

"Oh, man, How'd I get in this mess?! What a nightmare."

"Take it easy. I'm banking on keeping you alive if you cooperate with me. Brisco's banking on you dying whether you cooperate with him or not. Take your pick."

"All right. Anything else you want me to do?"

Yes, yes. I have a few questions about Brisco."

"Shoot . . . I mean 'go ahead."

"One, do you have any idea where he's staying in Newark, or what he's driving?"

"I'll try to find out, but, no, I don't have those answers."

"Okay, two, did he say anything about looking for me at my house?"

"No, but he does know where you live. I suspect he might have checked your place out and figured it would be better to meet up with you away from there. That's just my thought. Otherwise, why ask for places you might go to? Is that it?"

"Just two more.

"Go ahead."

"How did he seem on the phone: nervous, angry, tired, drugged out?"

"His normal self: bullish, no emotion in his voice."

"That's good to know. He'll be focused. He won't be doing anything rash. His plan to kill me will be calculated and executed with a bit more precision than the ones he planned against Marty."

"What happened with Marty?"

"Never mind. Now, to my last and most important question. Did he ask for any information on my wife or child, like where she works or where my daughter goes to play?"

"No, just about you."

"Good. And that's how you'll leave it. I know you're upset but try to relax. He'll be focused on me for the moment. Keep in touch. With any luck I'll let you know how my meeting went with him tomorrow at lunch."

9:50 AM
Lyndhurst/Bloomfield, New Jersey

"Jason, it's me."

"What's up, my brother?"

"I just got a call from a snitch I've been dealing with," said Mac. "He's been in touch with Brisco. I told him to tell Brisco I'm meeting you for lunch tomorrow at Giglio's on Bloomfield Avenue."

"You want me to meet you there? What time?"

"No, you stay put. I used your name, just to add a little more validity to the setup. He might have done some research on our family. It'd make sense that I'd be meeting *you* there."

"So, are you going to have anyone there for backup?"

"Yeah, I decided to let Arnet from Bergen County know. He's

got two murder cases where Brisco is suspect. He had put out a BOLO for him after the murders. Now that Florida put out an arrest warrant and APB for him, I think I'd better cover my bases and keep Arnet in the loop. With any luck, Brisco will show his hand. I don't suspect he'd want to be taken alive, not with all the jail time he's facing. So, with some backup, hopefully, he'll go down in a blaze of glory."

10:07 AM
Hackensack/Bloomfield, New Jersey

"Homicide Squad, Arnet."

"Hey, Lieutenant, Mac Taylor on this end. I need your help. I think you'll like what I'm offering." Mac then laid out the plan to meet with Brisco the next day around 12:30 at Giglio's.

"All right, Mac. I'm on board. I'll let the Essex County Prosecutor's Office and Bloomfield PD know that we'll be in the area tomorrow. They'll want to post some of their people at the scene. I'll make sure they're up to date on photos of Brisco, in case he slips the noose."

"Aah, don't talk like that Lieutenant. Think positive."

"I do, but I don't like surprises. Always have to be prepared for the unexpected."

"Good, then you'll want me to come by you early tomorrow to set up this meet."

"Yes, come early, about eight. I'll be here. Now I just have one big question for you."

"Go ahead, ask away."

"Who have you been talking to that has direct contact with Brisco? Someone who told him where you're going to be tomorrow?"

"Long story."

"I'm all ears."

"There's a kid named Alan Springer, who Brisco has been threatening to harm if he doesn't give him information on me, my family, Marty Presler, and his family. Springer came to me with his attorney out of 'good conscience'. Actually, the kid doesn't want to be killed by Brisco or me, should I find out he's giving him information. He'll cooperate with you but you know how civilians are, scared to testify against cons and ex-cons. That's him. And he doesn't want to get arrested for aiding or abetting a known fugitive, or conspiring to commit a crime. He's scared out of his sneakers. The only reason he got dragged into this mess is because the father of his ex-girlfriend had done time with Brisco. Her dad told Brisco that Springer can get info on anyone. And so the intimidation began. After tomorrow, I'll bring him to your office and let him tell his tale of woe. That is after we lock up that dirtbag Brisco, or put him out of his misery."

"Well, Mac, withholding information in a criminal investigation is not a good look for you. Nonetheless, if you bring me Brisco tomorrow, this can go away."

"Listen L.T., you were going nowhere with him. Marty and I made things happen in Florida that got an arrest warrant issued against him. It got his buddy arrested, who by the way, is cooperating with authorities down there. Plus, I arranged for this trap to be set for him in Bloomfield. So much for hindering a criminal investigation. Instead of looking to charge me, you should be pinning a medal on my chest. Stop thinking like a bureaucrat, and start thinking like a cop. We're all on the same team, just trying to survive and protect those who need protection. We do all we can do, not because we always like what we have to do but because we just *have* to do it. We are the last wall of defense on their behalf. We fall, this whole house of cards we call civil society falls."

"There's still a playbook that we have to go by, Mac. You apparently don't like to play by the rules. You should have brought this kid in earlier. This isn't just *your* case. It's mine, too."

"Was your life, or your family's life threatened in this case, L.T.?! I think I have a lot more at stake in this case than you do. You wanna charge me, charge me. Let's see how far that goes with a jury. Especially after hearing all the cooperation I've given you, with my life and my family's life on the line. Now, are you on board for tomorrow, or do you want me to handle this on my own . . . which personally, I'd prefer?"

"We're on. See you at eight."

7:02 PM
Orlando, Florida

An undercover ICE agent dressed in casual street clothes walked into Chicas, Chicas, Chicas and sat at the bar. He ordered a juice, paid for it, and tipped the barmaid a couple of dollars. He then handed her a ten-dollar bill for the topless, darkhaired young woman gyrating on stage to the Cuban music. The dancer put the ten in the garter belt on her thigh. Ten minutes later another undercover agent decked out in a torn t-shirt and faded shorts came in and sat down at the other end of the bar. He, too, ordered the customary juice and dropped a fifty-dollar bill on the bar. "Take ten for the drink, five for you, and ten for the lovely dancer. Leave the rest on the bar." The dark-haired dancer took the ten that was handed to her and placed it slowly in her G-string.

Approximately one-half hour later, in walked Sanchez. He approached a topless, buxom brunette carrying drinks to a nearby table.

"I'm here to see Maggie . . . or Benito," he said.

"Maggie's in the backroom. Who should I say is here?"

"Manny. I'm here for a mutual friend, Snake."

"I'll tell her you're here."

A minute later, Maglia "Maggie" Selina came by the front of the bar and met Sanchez. "So, you're Manny. Follow me."

Maggie led Sanchez to a U-shaped, red-padded booth by the rear of the bar. She sat across from him. Sanchez then took out an envelope containing three-thousand dollars in hundred-dollar bills and placed the envelope in front of her. Maggie picked up the envelope, took the cash out and counted it.

"It's all here," she said. "Now, tell me how do you know Snake?"

"I get my shit from him, have been for quite a while."

"What's your last name, Manny, and what do you do for a living?"

"It's Hernández, and I work with my dad."

"What do you and your dad do?"

"Financial stuff. Investment income, mostly corporate and pension money."

"All right, I'll let Mr. Valverde know you're here. He might want to talk with you." As Maggie got up to leave, Sanchez looked across the bar, trying not to stare at either of his two backup agents.

"Hello, Manny. I'm Benito Valverde. I'm glad you were able to help out our friend in this matter."

"Yeah, no problem. I've been dealing with Snake for a while. He's good on the money."

Valverde seemed taken aback for a moment. "You look familiar," he said. "Have I seen you before?"

Caught off guard by the question, Sanchez replied, "Could be." Then, in an attempt to mitigate the threat-felt inquiry, he added, "I've been in your club. I do business in Orlando. Snake told me the girls here are outstanding. I agree. Maybe you've seen me here before."

"Yeah, maybe that's it. I'm usually pretty good with faces. I'm surprised, though, that Snake never mentioned your name before, since you've been with him a while."

"I don't know. Maybe he likes to keep his buyers close to his vest. I haven't told anybody about my relationship with him. If a friend wants some dope, I'd tell 'em 'I got a guy,' but I'd never give them his name. I assumed that's how he would want it. I guess that's how it works the other way, too."

"Well, let's not talk about things like money or dope. I don't know anything about that. Who are you? I never heard Snake mention your name until the last call I had with him. He said you and your dad are in the financial investment business. Maggie just told me the same thing. Interesting. Tell me about your business. Do you handle a lot of individual investors?"

"Well, yes and no. We handle corporate money and pension funds. Big, big money there. My father, though, does do quite a bit of trading with high-end individual investors. We're talking in the fifty-million- plus-dollar range."

"What's the name of your company?"

Sanchez smiled. "I'll let you know if you decide to do business with us. We are a very private corporation."

Valverde gave Sanchez a long, hard stare.

"Does your dad do any off-shore investing?"

"Of course, moving that kind of money needs world-market access. Our clients are heavily invested in international and global funds. Also, private investments with foreign governments."

"Well, I suspect much of his work deals with sheltering money. Cash businesses are perfect for those so-called 'tax advantages'. Wouldn't you agree?"

"Of course. Your place is ideal for sheltering money. Plus, I don't know what other cash businesses you're in. Do you mean providing tax shelters . . . or are we talkin' 'laundering' your money?"

"Oh, that's such a nasty word 'laundering.' It's illegal, Manny," Valverde said with a smile.

"Well, there are ways to clean cash, legally."

"Really, how?"

"Briefly, open cash accounts in different countries, buy product and service companies here or abroad."

"Sounds simple enough."

"Well, there's more to it than that. Your money has to be packaged with money from other investors which makes it more difficult to trace."

"How would I get my money back then?"

"Several ways. You charge high fees for products and services from the company you invested in with overseas money. The money goes from your bank accounts abroad to your company accounts either here in the U.S. or abroad. Eventually, you sell your stake in the company."

"That's the payoff?"

"With high-profit margins, you can sell your stake to other buyers looking to clean some cash, or you can create sales invoices for your product or products without actually delivering any of it. That part, by the way, isn't legal. But, if you follow legal channels, you will have to pay taxes on the money. Granted you'll be paying income and capital-gains taxes on profits, but the original cash will grow and be clean. And the profits will be legal and plentiful. It's all about the placement of the funds, the blending, layering, and transferring of those assets with legit assets, and then the sale of those assets or the cancellation of agreements and repayment with legal sources."

"That's it?"

"That's it. Well, from our end, there's a lot of paperwork and legwork needed to be done: opening up accounts, transferring funds, investing in specific companies, just to name a few."

"And, of course, there's a fee for all that," Valverde noted.

"Of course. We're all in the business of making money. Our take is two percent of your cost basis and two percent of all profits from your investments. For example, invest one million dollars and pay us a separate twenty grand upfront. A somewhat conservative return on your investment is between five and ten percent. That's around fifty-to-one-hundred-thousand-dollar total profit. Your original one mil is clean and after paying us one to two K, you walk away with a net profit of around forty-nine to ninety-six thousand dollars. But more importantly, your one mil has been cleaned."

"You've given me something to think about, Manny. Your fees seem a bit steep, though."

"Our fees might seem high but what we do has substantial risks. Higher legal risks, higher profits, therefore higher fees."

"All right. Let me think about it. I'm glad I met you, Manny. Now I know why Ripper has kept you under wraps. Let's talk again. We might be able to do business."

17

AUGUST 20, 2015

11:45 AM
BLOOMFIELD, NEW JERSEY

Four undercover cops spread out along Bloomfield Avenue near Giglio's. Detective Lieutenant Arnet sat in an unmarked car a block away from the restaurant.

"All in position? Radio check," Arnet said into his portable unit.

They all responded by number—check—into their body microphones.

Numbers One and Two were Mac Taylor and the undercover who was to act as his lunch partner, Jason. After all units gave the okay, Mac and the undercover agent with him entered the restaurant. They asked to sit outside so all the undercovers could have a good look at them and anyone approaching them. Both Mac and the undercover sat at a 45-degree angle with their backs to the brick wall of the building. A large ceramic planter stood just inside the low metal fence that encircled the outside restaurant tables. As the two men carried on small talk, both had their handguns by their sides and ready to flip the table they were sitting at should the need arise. Besides their bulletproof vests, Mac and company figured they had enough cover with the table and planter should a gunfight arise.

Around 12:20, one of the undercover officers across the street noticed a well-built male walking solo up the street in the direction of the restaurant.

"Six to L.T. One male on foot, three stores down from restaurant. Okay to cross the street and follow."

"Stay put Six. Keep your area covered in case of a backup for this guy. Five, follow the target. Three, start moving toward the restaurant to intercept, if necessary."

"Six received. Five okay; Three on my way."

The targeted male kept his hands in his pockets as he slowly approached the restaurant.

"Three and Five, if the target moves toward our guys or starts to take his hands out of his pockets as he nears them, intercept. *He doesn't have a limp and doesn't look quite like recent photos of Brisco*, Arnet thought, *but we can't take the chance that he has someone else to do his dirty work; someone who has a better chance of getting close to Taylor without being noticed; who can put a bullet or two in him and walk away, to be picked up by a cohort.*

As the muscular male turned toward the entrance of the restaurant, Arnet called out on the radio, "Take him!"

Undercover Three closed in rapidly on the man, producing a badge in one hand and a gun in the other. Undercover Five moved in from behind, handgun held at a 45-degree angle to the ground.

"Whoa! What's going on?!" asked the target.

"Just step over here by the curb. No fast moves." Just then Arnet drove his vehicle to the front of the restaurant. Undercover Five patted down the target before placing him in the backseat of the car. The man was unarmed. Undercover Three also got in the back seat.

"Am I being arrested for something?! 'Cause I ain't done nothin'."

"Not at the moment," said Arnet. "We just have some questions that need to be answered."

"Like what?"

"Like your name, where you live, and where you were going when we stopped you."

"I don't have to tell you nothing. I didn't do anything."

"Your choice. We can go straight to police headquarters and see if you can give a good account for yourself because, you see, we have an ongoing investigation in which you might be considered a material witness. In which case, we'll be holding you until we can get those answers. Or, you can answer our questions now and go your own way. Your choice, the hard way or the easy way."

"All right, my name is Dillon Campo. I live over on Pulaski Street."

"What were you doing here on Bloomfield Avenue in Bloomfield?"

"Just looking to get something to eat."

"Have you been here before?"

"No."

"Do you eat alone often or were you meeting someone here?"

"I was just gonna get some pizza and then head home."

"Do you know a guy named Alex Brisco?"

"Brisco, Brisco? I don't think so."

"Now think about that. We'll be running checks. We'll find out if you're being square with us. I think we best go to police headquarters where these two gentlemen will run some checks."

"You said I could go if I answered some questions—which I did!"

"Yeah, well, I didn't like your answers."

"If I'm suspected of doing something illegal here, you're supposed to read me my rights."

"Mr. Campo," said Arnet. "You're not under arrest and you haven't been accused of a crime so there's no need to read you your rights."

"Then let me go."

"Remember what I said about being a material witness. Well, I think you might have information on Alex Brisco. So, you won't be going anywhere until we have a good, long talk with you."

Arnet put the gray sedan in gear and headed back to Bergen County.

12:10 PM
Bloomfield/Verona, New Jersey

Brisco watched from down the block as Arnet and company drove away with Campo in the back seat. He knew he was set up. *Glad I sent Ripper in first to test the waters. Springer has been playing me,* he thought. He then pulled out of his parking spot and headed north.

Once in Verona, Brisco turned his vehicle into a secluded area and put in a call on his cell phone to Alan Springer.

"Hello," said Alan Springer.

"You're dead!" was all Brisco said before disconnecting the call.

Springer immediately called him back. "I didn't tell anybody anything about you, Mr. Brisco. I swear, I wouldn't do that! I helped you out, right? I did everything you asked. I gave you information. Whatever you wanted. Whatever I could find on the people you were looking for."

"You set me up."

"No, no, you got that all wrong. I didn't know the cops were playing me. The email I hacked into saying Taylor was meeting someone named Jason had to have been planted by the cops. I was set up, too. Look, I don't know what bind you're in now but I have cash. I'll give you what money I have, if that will help. I have about one thousand two hundred dollars lying around. I don't trust banks. If you knew what I know, you wouldn't trust them either. Hackers can get into anyone's account if they try hard enough. Come see me. I have the money for you."

"Okay, kid. Have the money and meet me out front. I'm on the move, so I have no time to waste jabbering about who knew what."

"Thank you, sir. You know where I live, right? I'll be waiting in the driveway. I'll have the cash with me. You don't have to worry about me. I didn't know they set me up. Believe me, I didn't know."

Springer wasn't aware that Brisco had disconnected the call right after Springer said 'I'll be waiting in the driveway.'

12:14 PM
Newark, New Jersey

"Mac, it's me, Akins."

"Roger, what's up?"

"I just got a call from Alan. He said Brisco called and threatened to kill him."

"Well, get him the hell out of his house. ASAP! It's probably the only place Brisco knows about. He'd get that from either the ex-girlfriend or her father. Have him go somewhere neither of them know about. A friend maybe, coffee shop, preferably a police station."

"I know. I have to notify the police."

"Call him first. You can call the police after you call him. If he's got a gun, have him barricade himself in and wait for the police to arrive. Otherwise, have him head directly to the nearest police station. I can't head to where he is or will be going right now. Believe it or not, I was just about to meet up with Brisco but he slipped the noose. We are looking for a lead on him right now."

"So, that's why he'd been threatened. He worked something out with you. I don't have to guess now what triggered Brisco to threaten him?"

"First things first. Call Springer now! Tell him to get the hell out of his house now, if he's there! And don't play dumb with me, Roger. I suspect Springer told you why Brisco thinks he betrayed him. It has a lot to do with our failed attempt to get a piece of Brisco today. I told Alan to call him and tell him I was meeting someone for lunch in Bloomfield. We ultimately picked up a friend of Brisco's by the restaurant, but not him. He apparently suspected your client gave him the information in order to have him arrested. I'm running down leads now with Arnet of the Bergen County Homicide Squad. If I hear anything to help protect your client, I'll let you know. In the meantime, have him hunker down or go immediately to the PD to file a report. Don't waste any time. Call him back now! This guy Brisco is a psychopath. No telling what his next move might be."

"Okay, I'll call him back. Alan is scared to death right now."

"Okay, call me back after you contact him and the locals."

"I called him, Mac. He's going to the Verona PD. I'll meet him there," said Akins.

"Listen, Roger. This dirtbag should be heading out of the area. It's way too hot for him up here. That would be the smart thing to do, what a normal perp would do. But this nut job is anything but normal. I hope your client realizes that time is not on his side. If Brisco knows where he lives, he could be there at any moment."

"Let's hope not."

"Call Verona PD. Let them know to head over there, now! Just in case he's crazy enough to show up there. We'll call them from here, too."

"Look, I gotta go. Arnet just brought a friend of Brisco to his office. This guy Campo must be providing a place for him to stay. Brisco can't afford to hang around and hope this guy will zip his lip about him. So, without a place to stay and no hope of his buddy staying quiet, I'm sure he'll be gone from here. Let's hope he doesn't try to take out your client before he heads out, I'd say keep a gun handy, but I suspect Springer isn't a pro-gun kind of guy. Nevertheless, no need for a restraining order. There's an arrest warrant out for Brisco. If he's seen anywhere, he'll be picked up."

"Mac, I brought this guy to you to protect him from Brisco . . . and the police. Now I have no choice but have him report what he's been doing and why Brisco is after him. I thought you would have provided cover for him. I see you instead helped to set him up."

"Roger, your guy was giving Brisco info on me, my family, Marty and his family. I never planned on taking a bullet for him. We do have an oral agreement, though, so I will protect him the best I can. The plan was to get Brisco to the restaurant. He smelled a rat and sent in his decoy. We are oh for two now with him. The police that were involved in Venice, Florida, were an unforeseen circumstance. Marty and I had no idea Brisco was being tailed. And here in Bloomfield, getting the police involved was a mistake. If Brisco's not caught by cops on the beat, the next time *we* meet, it will only be him and me. That'd be it. No police posse."

"And what makes you think there'd be a next time?" asked Akins.

"There will be a next time. Mark my words on that."

"Well, our deal is off, Mac. Alan will be cooperating with the police from now on, not you. Forget his phone number. I was hoping you could keep him out of this, but instead you brought him deeper into the mix."

"Life sucks, doesn't it? It was your client who was dealing with Brisco. That was his first mistake. Second mistake, not going directly to the police because you were afraid they'd charge him for suspected hacking offenses. Third mistake, coming to me and expecting me to place a higher regard on his life than that of my family, my friend, and my friend's family. You've spent too much time in the courtroom and with your nose in the books. There is a serial killer out there, and he's not going to stop until he *is* stopped. Having your guy Springer help set up Brisco was the best opportunity we had to grab him. I'd do it again, if I had the opportunity, only the next time without all the backup."

"Well, good luck on your hunting expedition," said Akins. "Meanwhile, I'll be calming down my client. You know, the one you were supposed to help."

"Just something to remember, Roger. Your client was going to be a target whether or not he agreed to help him. It appears Brisco has a long memory, and he always tries to wipe his slate clean. Another psycho, Albert Anastasia of Murder Incorporated—reportedly responsible for the killer of over 750 individuals—was quoted as saying, "Ya got no witness, ya got no case!" Your boy was, and is, a witness, whether you like it or not. With or without me, Brisco won't forget that."

Mac hung up.

1:20 PM
Bergen County Prosecutor's Office
Hackensack, New Jersey

"Campo, Campo," Arnet said as he looked down on the printout in front of him. "Dillon Campo, aka Ripper. Seven years in Trenton State for three armed robberies and aggravated assault. Looks like an assortment of other offenses and jail time for gun possession, domestic violence, burglary and theft. An impressive résumé."

Arnet put down the rap sheet. "And you want to tell us that you don't know Alex Brisco, aka Bull, who you spent time with in Trenton State."

"I spent time with a lot of guys in prison. I don't remember them all."

Arnet smiled. "But you just happened to be in downtown Bloomfield at the exact time and place Brisco was to show up."

"Sounds like a coincidence to me," said Campo.

"I don't believe in coincidences," said Arnet. "I believe in complicity. And right now I have you complicit in planning to commit murder."

"What?! You can't lay a murder rap on me. I was just walking down the street."

"Well," said Arnet, "we have evidence that your pal Brisco has killed several people, and has made attempts to kill several more individuals . . . and he was planning to kill one of those individuals today at the exact location you just happened to pass by and at the exact time the murder was to take place. I'd call that aiding and abetting a murder suspect."

"You've got nothin' on me. I want an attorney. I know my rights."

"You can go get yourself an attorney if you'd like. You're not under arrest. You free to go at any time. Just know this. We do our homework. We now know where you've been living. We'll be getting your phone records to see who you've been speaking with. We'll have eyes on you 24/7. Right now, we're just finishing up on a search warrant for your girlfriend's house. We suspect she's been harboring Brisco, a known fugitive, friend of yours."

"She's got nothing to do with Brisco!" Campo shot back.

"Ah, now you remember his name. Maybe she doesn't have anything to do with him," said Arnet, "but if he was or is there, fingerprints will be found. If not prints, we still might find drugs or illegal contraband. It's not going to look good for your girlfriend."

"I'm going right now to stop any illegal search of her apartment."

"Yeah, that's not a good idea. It's just going to get you arrested for interfering with a police investigation. And while you're in jail, your girlfriend might soon be joining you."

"Okay, what do you want from me?"

"I want to know everything you know about Brisco. Where he is, what's his next plan."

"Are you still going to search my girlfriend's apartment?"

"Absolutely, but she can be spared it all if you take the rap for protecting your buddy Brisco. She's collateral damage right now, but you can man up and admit it was all you. Otherwise, she takes the fall, too. I suspect her defense would be that it was all you anyway, so why not save us the bullshit. If you do, the prosecutor might give you a sweatheart deal—no pun intended—for your cooperation."

"Leave her out of this, and I'll tell you what you wanna know. That's the deal. And no harboring, known associations, abetting, complicity, or any other bullshit charges against her or me."

"I'll talk to the prosecutor, but he'll first want your cooperation. You do well, and we should have a deal. Are you ready to talk?"

1:30 PM
Verona, New Jersey

"You, you son-of-a-bitch! I trusted you!"

"Who the hell is this!"

"It's me, Roger, Roger Akins. Verona P.D. just found my client Alan Springer's body under some bushes by his house. He was shot and killed, after I told him to meet me at the police station. Had I gone to pick him up, I would be dead right now, too. I never should have trusted you!"

Silence.

"Hello?" said Akins. "Are you listening? Alan is dead! The shooter is gone. We know who the shooter is, don't we, Mac? Nice job protecting 'my boy.'"

Silence again.

"Are you listening to what I'm saying?"

"Wow, that psychopath has to be stopped."

"You think?" Akins said sarcastically.

"Let me ask you one question, counselor. Why did it take so

long for Springer to leave his house? You called *me* over an hour ago. Brisco couldn't have gotten there that fast. And he wasn't going to wait outside long with every cop looking for him. He had to think that his car was possibly IDed through Campo. What's missing here? You're not telling me the whole story."

Dead air.

"So, Roger, he found out rather quickly where Springer lived."

"I guess, like you said, the father of that girlfriend or former girlfriend of his—you know, the guy Brisco spent time with—must have told him. I suspect Brisco had been waiting by Springer's place when he called. He probably coaxed him around the corner of the house, shot him, and hid the body before taking off. The cops must've just missed him."

"Then he should have listened to me before this meet was to go down. He could have gone to the police anytime. That's on you, not me. And how did he know Springer was going to come out of his house at that exact time? What's going on? I'm not that gullible."

"Okay, okay. After I called him, Alan said he was going to call Brisco back and plead with him. He was going to offer him all the cash he had to help him get away and leave him alone. I guess Brisco agreed, met Alan, took the money, and shot him anyway."

"Did you advise him to do that, Roger?"

The phone went dead.

2:30 PM
NEWARK, NEW JERSEY

The manhunt reached several dead ends, beginning with the search warrant at Campo's girlfriend's house along with the corresponding Florida and New Jersey arrest warrants for Alex Brisco. Although there were no eyewitnesses to the Springer shooting, the Essex County Prosecutor felt, based on the reported verbal threats to kill reported by the victim to fresh witnesses Mac Tayler and Roger Akins, there was enough probable cause to add another murder charge against Brisco. The County Prosecutor banked on telephone and computer records to collaborate witness claims. The murder and attempted murder counts against Brisco kept piling up.

2:41 PM
East Orange/Weehawken, New Jersey

Brisco found a secluded street by the Garden State Parkway. He dumped the car between two parked vehicles. He then popped the trunk, took out a hat, sunglasses, a syringe, and a vial of Deca-Durabolin, his 'roid of choice. He tapped the handgun beneath the front of his untucked shirt, then felt in his left pocket for the one thousand two hundred thirty-five dollars in cash that Springer gave him before taking a bullet to the head. Brisco then sat down behind a bush by the side of a neighborhood home and shot up. Leaving the syringe and empty ampul by the bush, he walked down several houses to a traffic light.

At the light, Brisco saw an elderly man seated in a light-blue Honda Accord waiting for the light to turn green. He knocked on the passenger window. The man rolled it down.

"Can I help you?"

Brisco pulled out his gun and placed his hand inside the window. With his other hand, he opened the passenger door and got in. "Just drive where I tell you."

The driver started gasping for breath. "Please don't shoot me! Take my car. I'll get out now."

Pointing the gun at the driver, Brisco said, "Just shut up and drive."

"Where?!"

"Get over to 495 and head east. I'll tell you when to pull over.

You'll be fine as long as you do what I say. Got it?"

"Yeah, sure. But you can have the car now. I won't report anything if you just let me go."

"Shut up and do what I tell you. You'll be okay. Believe me. Just drive."

The man then headed to Route 495.

At the Imperial Port in Weehawken, Brisco told the driver to pull into the parking garage. "Go to the roof," he ordered.

Once on the top level, Brisco moved to the back seat still threatening the driver with his gun. He waited until a driver a few spaces away parked his car and headed for the elevator. Once he was gone, Brisco removed his belt.

"You'll be okay," he said to the driver. "This will all be over soon." With that, he wrapped the belt around the driver's neck. The driver kicked and pulled on the belt, but Brisco was too strong for him to pull it off. He tried to scream but the belt kept tightening around his neck and all that he could get out were some garbled words. In a very short time, the driver purged what little air was left in his mouth and slumped back in his seat. Brisco reached over the seat and pushed him down. He then returned to the front seat and went through the victim's pockets. He found some cash, a wallet with ID in it, and a shopping list. He hunkered down in the car until dark, at which time he drove to meet his friend Mike.

8:43 PM
Weehawken, New Jersey

"Hey, Mike," Brisco said as his cell buddy opened the door.

"Wow, man. Bull. What brings you here? And at this time? Who ya runnin' from?"

"Long story. I need a favor."

"Come in, come in."

Once inside, Brisco went into the living room and peeked out the curtain overlooking the street. "Let me park my car along the back of your house. Ya gotta open the gate."

"Sure," Mike Alfonso said. He then went and slipped a pair of pants on under his robe, and placed his house slippers back on.

The two left the house. Alfonso unlocked the gate as Brisco backed up and pulled the Accord down the side of the house and parked it around back. The two then went in the back door.

"What's up, Bull? You know I've been clean for a long time. I just did you a favor. I gave you the number of my daughter's ex-boyfriend. I hope he was helpful."

"Well, that's another story. Look, Mike, I need to wash up, and I need some food, some clothes, and if you've got some pick-me-ups, I can use them. I've got a long trip ahead of me."

"Sorry, no drugs, but I have a shirt that will fit you, and a baseball cap . . . blue with the Mets logo on it." Alfonso smiled at that last remark. Brisco didn't.

"Listen, go upstairs and clean up. When you come down, I'll have some cheese sandwiches for you. Not much else in the fridge. Do you like cheese?"

"Yeah, sure. I'd eat shoe leather right now, I'm so hungry. I haven't eaten or drank a thing since this morning."

Brisco finished taking a shower and put on the fresh shirt and socks Alfonso gave him. He went downstairs and had a beer and a cheese sandwich with Mike. He then packed up two more sandwiches, several bottles of water, and two beers for the road trip south.

"I had a rough day," he said to Alfonso.

"Don't want to hear it, Bull. Don't want to be complicit in any of your latest ventures. Like I told you last time, 'I'll help you out but I don't want to be a part of any of your dealings. I'm not going back in. I did enough jail time. So, good luck, wherever you're headed."

"All right, I hear what you're saying. But me, I still have some scores to settle."

"Just be careful who your scores are. Remember the major league pitcher Satchel Paige. He said, "Don't look back; something might be gaining on you.' Words of wisdom, Bull. Don't look back."

"Don't worry 'bout me. I'll be fine. Love to continue this conversation, but I gotta get goin'. I got a long trip south ahead of me. Now, before I leave, I just need two more items."

9:47 PM
Bayonne, New Jersey

Brisco drove to a secluded area by the Hudson River and dumped the body that he placed earlier in the trunk of the car, in the water. He then searched the area for a similar looking vehicle. He didn't see any light-blue Honda Accords, but he did see a midsized-blue colored Chevy Impala. Not nearly the same but close enough. Not that it mattered. If a cop ran the plate on his car, he knew it wouldn't match up. But it didn't matter because he knew once the police realized the car was stolen, they'd look for the plate number on the passing and parked vehicles. So, he quickly switched plates using the screwdriver and pliers Alfonso gave him.

10:42 PM
Lyndhurst/Bloomfield, New Jersey

Mac holstered both his handguns and loaded luggage in his truck. He drove to Jason's house where Cheryl and Hope were staying.

"So, you're off again," said Cheryl.

"According to Brisco's pal, Campo, he should be heading back to Florida. That's where his major contacts are. He has nowhere to go up here; no place to stay. They just found his car in East Orange by the Parkway. That means he either physically carjacked or hotwired a vehicle, or he had somebody he knows help him escape. Campo doesn't know of anyone up here that would do that for him. That's why Brisco stayed with him and his girlfriend. But he did say Brisco kept a lot to himself. Plus, he's very persuasive. No telling what his options might be. In any event, the state police are on high alert for him, particularly along the Garden State Parkway and the I95 corridor. And, I let Marty know to keep an eye out for him and that I'll be heading back down."

"Sounds like a long way to go with every law enforcement agency looking for him."

"Let's just hope no one else gets killed along the way by this lunatic. Any cop pulling him over better have backup 'cause Brisco will waste no time pulling the trigger. This guy's got a death wish. He knows he can't keep running like this. He's already left a trail of dead bodies. What's a few more? He's gotta know his luck is bound to run out."

"You are now scaring me, Mac. Why not let the weight of the law catch up with him instead of you always having to take care of business. You did your job years ago when you arrested him and had him put away. The system let him back out. Let the system put him back in now."

"Unfortunately, Cheryl, the system depends on people like me and Marty, Arnet and McDaniel, and those ICE agents we dealt with in Florida to do the job. We're the part of the system that prevents anarchy and chaos out there."

"So, I guess you're always going to be the guy wearing the white hat. When are you going to call it quits and just be a regular husband and father?"

"When I get back, honey. I promise."

Cheryl lowered her eyebrows and smirked. "Yeah, right" was her reply.

"I said, 'I promise'."

"Your promises don't mean much anymore, Mac. You promised to give up this thing after the last time you ran around Pennsylvania, Ohio, and Paris, France."

"What would you have me do, Cheryl, let this murderer stalk you and Hope, your brother and his family, my buddy Marty?"

"Let the police handle it! You're not the police anymore!"

"It's in my blood, Cheryl. What can I say? This guy Brisco is a physical threat to all the people I know. I can't just sit by and let the police, who have no personal stake in this game, handle this."

"Well, I'm tired of this whole situation. It was one thing when only our lives were at stake, even when I was pregnant and that maniac tried to kill me. But now Hope is in the picture, and I want her to have a normal life, not running from psychopaths every other day."

"A normal life? Tell that to Brisco's victims. You can't Cheryl, because some of them are dead, and the ones who survived are scarred for life. The normal lives of the dead ones ended quite brutally and for those still around, their normal lives turned into nightmares. No one is guaranteed a normal life."

"I know that, Mac. But my point is I don't want *our* lives to end either of those ways. And the way you continue to fight whatever demons are floating around in your head, I'm becoming more and more assured that one of those ways is going to be the end result."

"It's not going to happen, Cheryl. I've got it covered. You know that."

"I know nothing of the sort. You live in a very dangerous world, Mac. One that never seems to get better. If you leave to run after this nut case looking to kill you, don't expect me and Hope to be here when you get back. I don't know where we'll be but it won't be at Jason and Ann's house. They have enough to worry about with their kids. They don't need me hanging around their necks like an albatross."

"I'm sorry, Cheryl. I can't help who I am. I can't rest knowing this animal is still out and about, killing people randomly and wanting to kill me, my family, and my brother officer's family. It's in my nature."

"Just like the scorpion, Mac. If you remember, it didn't end well for it, either."

Mac went to kiss Cheryl goodbye. She turned her head. But as he walked away, she said, "You know I love you."

"Yeah, I do," he replied. He then went into Hope's bedroom, kissed her, and left. But instead of immediately heading south, he returned to his home in Bloomfield.

Mac entered his office, turned on the lights, and reached into his desk.

Pulling out his pad, Mac went through the notes of his interview with Alan Springer. Not much to be learned on the credit card Brisco was using. He'd be dealing in cash right now. Springer didn't offer any background information on Brisco . . . other than his relationship with the father of Springer's ex-girlfriend. He apparently had done prison time with Brisco. Mac turned a page. There it was. *Ex-girlfriend Jean. Dad Mike Alfonso.*

Mac then scanned through his Internet P.I. criminal and civil websites and learned that a Michael Alfonso (DOB. 4/16/53), aka Miguel Alfonso and Al Fonso, lived in a one-family home in Weehawken with Jean (Alfonso/Debois) Colaneri and her husband Frank. His criminal record revealed that Alfonso's crimes consisted of several counts of aggravated assaults, arson, and extortion. He had, however, been out and about in society for the last several years without any further reported incidents. Knowing criminals of that caliber, however, Mac was not sure how accurate that blank slate could be. He was about to find out.

18

AUGUST 21, 2015

12:52 AM
WEEHAWKEN, NEW JERSEY

"Are you Mike Alfonso?" Mac asked as the powerful looking 61-year-old man opened the door.

"And who might you be? Don't you know what time it is?!'"

"I'm an acquaintance of Alan Brisco. Do you have a moment to talk?"

"Talk about what?"

"About your buddy, Bull."

"Get outta here." Alfonso then went to close the door.

Mac put his left foot between the door and the doorjamb. With his right hand and shoulder, he pushed the door hard against Alfonso. Then, with his left hand, he reached around back and pulled out his Glock .45.

"Wow, Jack!" Alfonso said as he backed away from the gun. "I don't know who you are, what Brisco has to do with you, or what you think I know about him."

"Back off and have a seat on your couch. Where's your daughter Jean? Where's Frank? Anybody else living here?"

"Nobody's here, just me. They don't live here anymore. How do you know about them?"

"I'll ask the questions," Mac said. "Brisco. Was he here? Did he stop by for any reason in the last day or so?"

"Who the hell are you?"

"There's a bullet in this gun with your name on it. Ask me one more time, and you'll buy it. Now answer the question! I do have some answers, so if you answer the question wrong, you will buy that bullet."

"Okay. Okay. I know the guy. I spent time with him in the pen. I guess you know that, that's why you're here. Since he's been out, he called me for a favor."

"What was that favor?"

"He told me he needed some info on some people, and if I knew how to get that info. I told him my daughter was separated from her first husband and was dating some young, computer geek. I told her a friend of mine was looking for information and that I needed her boyfriend's telephone number. She gave it to me, and I gave it to Bull."

"Well, just so you know. That kid is dead. Brisco shot him. He killed at least two other people, and I suspect he carjacked someone, who's probably also dead by now. I'm here to administer some justice for those deaths. Which means I'm going to kill him and anyone who stands in my way. So, here's the deal. You give me the information I need, and you live. You don't, you die. Capisci?!"

"Look, I've been threatened many times before. I've never had a cop threaten me with death, though. So, I suspect you're not one of those lowlifes. I gotta believe you're serious about shooting me; though, I don't know what Bull has to do with you . . . unless, of course, you're one of the guys he's after."

"You guessed it. Now answer my questions, or you'll be a casualty for Brisco's side of the ledger. First question, was Brisco here recently, like the last two days?"

"He was here a while ago. He needed to wash up, have a change of clothes, pack some food. I gave him some cash."

"How long ago, exactly?"

"Hours ago. I don't know exactly how long ago."

"Last night?"

"Yeah, last night."

"Don't play with me," said Mac. "What time last night?"

"I guess around ten, nine-thirty, ten."

"Did he say where he was headed?"

"I think he said he was heading south. He didn't say where south, but that's what I got from our conversation."

"Did he say how he was going to get there?"

"I guess drive. He had a car with him."

"Were you able to determine the make, model, or color of the car?"

"I noticed the car was some blue-colored, mid-sized car. Not sure of the make, could have been a Ford, Chevy, or maybe even one of those foreign models. Can't say for sure."

"Anything else I should know about before I track him down and kill him. You'd want to let me know, because If I find out you gave him something else like a car, a weapon, or a stolen credit card, I will be back. And you will be put on my hit list."

"Look, the only other things I gave him beside the food and some clothes was a screwdriver and a pair of pliers. I have no idea what he needed them for but I gave them to him anyway."

5:03 PM
Orlando, Florida

"Candy, here's the drinks for the table in the back," said Maria from behind the bar.

Jill Morgan, aka Candy, was topless. Her outfit for the evening was a G-string, garter belt, and a pair of black leather heels. That was it.

She took the tray of drinks from the bar that surrounded the elevated dance floor and brought them to a table in the back where two Hispanic men were seated.

"Thank you, Cariña," said one of the two as she placed the drinks on the table. "What's your name?"

"Candy."

Pulling out a five-dollar bill, he said, "For you, Candy." She took the five and placed it in her garter."

"Now, do me a favor, por favor. Tell Mr. Valverde, that Manny is here to see him."

Jill Morgan then went to the back room where Maggie was doing some paperwork.

"There are two guys out front who say they are here to meet Mr. Valverde. One is named Manny."

"Two? I know Manny is supposed to be coming today. Don't know who this other person is. Let me go see what the story is first before I let Mr. Valverde know. He's not going to meet with anyone he doesn't know without a good explanation."

Maggie then walked to the table where the two men were seated.

"Hello, Manny." Then, looking at the man sitting across from him, she said, "Who's your friend?"

ICE Undercover Agent Anthony Banfield reached out to shake Maggie's hand. "I'm Randell Hart, I'm the chief financial officer at Worldwide Financial. Manny told me Mr. Valverde might be interested in investing money with us. I'm here with Manny to offer him a business proposition. A very safe and profitable one at that."

"Well, I handle all of Mr. Valverde's businesses, so I suspect he'll want me present during any negotiations."

"Works for us," said Banfield, hoping the hidden mic on him

caught that admission, even with the loud music playing in the background. "We're here to discuss his investment possibilities with our company."

"Okay. Let's go in the back. Follow me," Maggie said as she led the two undercover ICE agents into the backroom. "I'll get Mr. Valverde. Be right back."

A few minutes later, Valverde came up the basement stairs and entered the room.

"So, this is one of your business partners, Manny. You told me about your dad, but not about a partner of yours."

"Randell here has been with my dad's firm for some time now. He runs all financial operations. He's helped me with my clients to meet their needs. I'm a meet-and-greet kinda guy. Randell is *thee* technical guy. He moves the money around. He can answer any questions you might have about how our system works and how you can 'clean up' some things that need to be cleaned up. Need I say more?"

"You've said enough for the moment," said Valverde as he sized-up Banfield. He was dressed neatly, wearing a pair of soft-leather loafers, a casual pair of black slacks, an open-collared, white shirt, and a navy-blue sports jacket.

Valverde wasn't quite sure this guy was legit. He turned to Sanchez, "If we're going to talk business, I want my men to pat you two down. Just a precaution. You understand, right?"

"Yeah sure, Mr. Valverde. We understand. Right, Randell?"

Banfield nodded. "Yeah, knock yourself out. We don't want any conversation we have here to bite us in the ass. I'm not sure *you* don't have a bug around here. My boss wouldn't be happy knowing that either. He knows a lot of people, too, who wouldn't be happy knowing that. If you know what I mean."

"You come to see me, and you make threats."

"No threats. Just good business practices."

The undercover police unit outside monitoring the conversation told the other undercover units in the area to be ready to enter the club in case Banfield was found to be wired, or if Valverde took the perceived threat to a higher level.

Two of Valverde's muscle were summoned into the room. "These are my two best bodyguards," Valverde said, a smile crossing his face. "Don't be too rough with them, boys."

Jake and Angelo patted down both undercovers from top to bottom: hair, back, chest, stomach, waist, thighs, ankles, and feet.

"Nothing but wallets, keys, and cell phones," said Jake.

The microphone/transmitter located in the fake cellphone on Banfield's waist went undetected.

"Happy," asked Sanchez as the two men who patted him and Banfield down indicated that they were clean.

"Yes, I am," said Valverde.

"I guess it's my turn now," said Banfield. "We can offer you some great opportunities, but just so it's a level playing field, would you mind if we move to a booth in the back behind the bar and the dance floor? I'd feel a little more comfortable talking there without the possibility of us being taped and without your 'two best bodyguards' looming over us."

"Okay. But you'll have ten minutes to make your case, or my men will be obliged to walk you out."

"Mr. Valverde, I'm sorry we got off on the wrong foot," said Sanchez. "Randell is all business. Always has been. That's why he's our top guy in the firm, next to me and my dad, of course. Let's forget all this back and forth, and let's talk business."

Valverde, Maggie Selina, Sanchez, and Banfield left the backroom and sat in a secluded spot far from the end of the bar. Under orders from Valverde, Angelo went to cover the front door, and Jake went to lower the volume on the jukebox.

Banfield began. "Mr. Valverde, Manny tells me you might be

interested in investing some cash in our firm. I suspect he told you we are a large, private company. Very low key. We only handle high-end investors, those looking to invest fifty mil or more. I'm not sure you qualify. From what I see, you own a club. That alone won't cut it. But Manny tells me you have other stakes and interests. And that you might be looking to clean some large sums of cash. I have no idea where this additional revenue flow comes from. None of my business. I don't care. I just need to know if you can meet our minimum investment requirements."

"Oh, I can meet your requirements. But before I give you any information, I need to know who the hell you are? What's your company name?"

"Fair enough. We're called Worldwide Financial. As I said, we're a private company. We're not on any stock exchange. Going public attracts too much attention, too much accountability."

"Okay, you need to know my interests. It's all public record. I have two clubs, two massage parlors, and two escort services. I have several other investment interests that I'm not going to discuss with either of you right now."

Banfield looked at Sanchez. "Well, I guess that's it." He then stood up, offered a handshake to Valverde, and said, "Pleasure meeting you."

Valverde didn't shake his hand, instead pointed to the seat Banfield had been sitting in and said, "Sit back down. I have a few questions for you. One, how does your company turn my money into clean cash?"

Banfield sat back down. "What we do is establish several accounts for you, here and overseas. We put smaller amounts of cash in each account under bank regs that require government notifications. Then smaller amounts are continuously deposited in the domestic and overseas accounts and used to buy foreign currencies. The foreign currencies are then used to purchase legal, safe securities, such as blue-chip or value stocks, or used for loans, or payments for legit goods and services. A lot of money can be used to purchase real-estate overseas. We have many ways to clean money."

"What's your vig? Your fee?"

"Three to four percent. One to two percent upfront and two percent of the profit extracted. For example, you invest one-mil, we charge ten to twenty K. You extract, say 1.1 mil, we charge two K, two percent only on the hundred-thousand-dollar profit. The million has already been charged the initial fee."

"That's not what your partner here told me. He said you take two percent upfront. No mention of a one percent initial fee. No change on the, as you say, the extraction of cash. Why the difference in the front load?"

Looking back and forth, Banfield lowered his head. "Well, with all due respect to Manny, he's referring to a two percent initial fee that is for one to five mil investments. Five to ten mil is one and a half. Above ten is one percent. I'm not sure what category you'd fit into. You tell me."

Valverde ignored the response. "Your tail end fee of two percent still seems high," he said.

"Not really. Not considering the establishment of accounts, the transferring of payment, stock purchase transaction fees, transacting loan agreements, etcetera. Not to mention the criminal liability. Pretty reasonable fee, if you ask me. Now if you don't want to go that route, we have some big commercial real-estate clients who do have these accounts. They're always looking to sell properties and hide some of the money in sales from taxes. For example, they sell you a piece of property listed at three million dollars. You agree to purchase the property for 2.5 million dollars, not three mil. You put down some legit cash for a binder and down payment, and take a mortgage from us or one of our clients on the 2.5 mil balance owed.

Then, unbeknownst to the IRS, you give the seller five hundred K in cash, under the table, as the saying goes. That five hundred K is cash you need to clean up. The seller saves on five hundred K real estate tax and you unload five hundred K of dirty cash that turns into a brick-and-mortar asset. Keep the property, collect income off it, take tax deductions off it, or simply turn around and sell it. Either way, your five hundred thousand in cash has been cleaned.

And don't worry about the seller. Not that you would. That individual will be shuffling that five hundred thousand through various banks, loan agencies, and real-estate properties making more money off it. It's a win-win for all parties."

"I like the concept. But I need to think about it. Ya see, I don't trust anybody. Especially people I don't know. And I don't know you. And I never heard of your company. What's your company's name again?"

"Worldwide Financial."

"Well, before I dig into my pocket, I'm going to dig into all the Internet has to offer me on Worldwide Financial. So, for now, why don't you two just sit back and enjoy the entertainment. "

19
AUGUST 22, 2015

9:08 AM
ICE HEADQUARTERS
MIAMI, FLORIDA

"We gave it our best shot," said Sanchez, "but he didn't bite."

"I thought he'd commit to something—drugs, girls, prostitution, cash needed cleaning . . . anything," said Banfield. "He did slip that one time, though, when he said he had several other investment interests he was not going to discuss with us. That's when I got up to leave hoping he'd give us something to hang our hats on. But didn't. I was surprised when he pointed to have me sit back down. I thought that time we were going to get something useful out of him."

"He knows the game. Valverde keeps everything close to his vest," said Cabrero. "We better start drafting some paper on his place now, even though we have little probable cause."

"What the hell p.c. *do* we have?" said Banfield. "There's nothing to hang our hats on with the wires."

"We have a statement from Ramirez," said Sanchez, "that Valverde has been dealing drugs and transporting underaged girls across the State of Florida for illicit purposes. We can get a search warrant for his places based on Ramirez's report. Even though

Ramirez will be listed in the warrant with only a C.I. number, Valverde will know it was him who gave him up. Still, we have no choice if Valverde is sex-trafficking young girls and women. It's 'the greater good' argument. If we have to throw Ramirez to the wolves, so be it. After all, he's not Joe Blow, Model Citizen. And there might be some girls and women in Valverde's clutches who might very well need our help. Plus, there's the drug angle. If we find any on premises that would be a bonus."

"Yup, and we could get some real actionable intelligence from the employees," Banfield noted. "I personally want to have a sit down with that muscle head, Jake. I'd like to be the one to flip him and throw him in lockup, if we can get anything on him."

"And I want to have a talk with Maggie," said Sanchez. "She seems to know an awful lot about the Valverde enterprise. She did say that she was involved in all his business dealings."

Cabrero chimed into the conversation. "All right, guys. Let's start working on this warrant. I suspect Valverde will find out soon enough that Worldwide Financial has nothing to do with us, if the company exists at all."

"Boy, would I have loved for him to have made one admission of illegal behavior or activity on our tape. That would have corroborated what Ramirez has said, and it would have strengthened our warrant considerably. Nevertheless," said Sanchez, "we should be able to get a judge to sign it. Fingers crossed."

10:30 AM
Sarasota, Florida

Mac drove through the night, stopping only for gas and an occasional rest area. He arrived at Marty Presler's house and told him about the aborted attempt to catch Brisco and the killing of Springer. "Any new development down here?" he asked.

"Those Fed guys we dealt with are shaking the bushes around Miami and Orlando. Brisco could be at either location. I'm still on his target list, so I suspect he might be around here, too."

"So, no leads on where he might be holing up?"

"The Feds have a snitch in custody who apparently had Brisco staying with him before all this shit broke. He's been supplying them with information on a Cuba strip-club trafficker in Miami who had hired him and Brisco to do some muscle work. The perp also has a club in Orlando and several other holdings. They're more concerned with nailing their trafficking target than they are with nailing Brisco. They had their opportunities to get our boy in the past—before they learned about the murders—but they preferred to surveil him rather than arrest him."

"Well, Brisco threatened you, me, and our families. He killed three people that we know of right now. As far as I'm concerned, all other targets are collateral at this point. Let's head to this strip club in Miami or the one in Orlando. No games any more. This guy will tell us what we want to know."

"Or?"

"Or I'll slit his throat and anyone else who gets in our way."

"Mac, now you're being a bit extreme."

"Marty, the world we live in is a jungle, an anarchy. Kill or be killed. Be a predator or a prey. Civilized society is a façade, just wishful thinking. It's been that way for us our entire lives. I don't like it, but that's our reality. The animals we've dealt with in the past, on 'the Job', were cancer. Nothing's changed. The cancer continues, and the only way to stop it from spreading is to destroy it, to cut it out."

"You okay, my brother?" asked Presler. "I don't like hearing you talk like that. Don't let the dark side of life get you down. We have a lot to be thankful for—family, friends, our health, to name a few. Isn't that what it's all about?"

"Yeah, plus all the bullshit! Love your friends and family, but kill all your enemies. Isn't *that* what it's really all about? Isn't that the meaning to all this crap?"

"Don't you get it, Mac? *We* are the meaning to it all. Without us, nothing has meaning. Without having some values, some standards, it remains an ugly, God-forsaken place out there."

"Look around, my friend. It's never going to stop being a very ugly, God-forsaken place."

"Not by my standards."

"Marty, Marty, face it. It doesn't end well for any of us. It's just a matter of time. So, in the meantime, I'm going to fight this cancer. It will win in the end, we all die, but until that day comes, I'm going to attack it wherever it raises its deformed head. And right now, its head appears to have popped up in Cuban strip clubs in Miami and Orlando. I'm going to decapitate that whole crew for good. That's my next move. Just let me know if you're onboard."

"I'm with you on Brisco. But I didn't join 'the Force' to act as its chief executioner. We've stretched the law from time to time, but random killings were never in my playbook. I'll help you squeeze this guy from Miami, but I'm not in on your plan to kill him if he doesn't cooperate. That's mob shit. It's stepping over the line. It's the stuff we fought against our whole career."

"Well, maybe you, but not me. When the rules didn't apply to them, they didn't apply to me. And I made it this far."

"Yeah, on a wing and a prayer. You skated on those charges at that pond in New York State, and somehow made it through that trip to Paris. This is different, though, Mac. The Feds are surveilling these clubs, and they want this trafficker alive, to dig deeper into the organization and take it all down. If you, we, interfere with their investigation, there ain't no coming back from that."

"Believe me, I hope they can clean out that rats' nest they're working on, but, right now, I'm focused on Brisco, and anyone harboring him or who has knowledge of his whereabouts. They will pay a serious price if they don't come clean. Trust me on that."

"Including murder?"

"It's not murder. *You* call it murder. I call it justice."

"You call it what you want, but random killing people is murder in my book."

"I'm not going to randomly kill anyone. If and when it's killing time, I'm only going to take out the ones who deserve it."

"I hear you, brother, but I've got to beg off this plan of yours."

"So, you're out?"

"Yep. Sorry, Mac. I've been with you since we started out in patrol. We've been partners for a long time. I'd do anything for you. Anything, but not wholesale killing. And that is what this would be. I'm in for going after Brisco. After all, he's going after us. But barging into a strip club, shooting bouncers, patrons, and the owner because they won't give, or don't have, information on Brisco, is more than I want to deal with. That's what the cartels would do. We'd be no better than them."

"I'm sorry, too, Marty. Sorry that you won't have my back on this. We have to take out Brisco in any way we can. We have no choice. If I'm forced to play by his rules—that being no rules—then anyone caught in the crossfire is just collateral damage."

"And killing anyone who just happens to get caught up between you, me, and Brisco is a price *I'm* not willing to pay."

"Well, good luck sitting here and waiting for Brisco to strike. Sounds like your plan is a dead end to me, the operative word being 'dead'. I, on the other hand, plan to go on offense. I'll be heading to Miami first. The scum bucket who's running the strip club, employing Brisco, and trafficking in God knows what—drugs, women, guns—is going to find out what it's like to be on the short end of the stick. Be well, my brother. I'll let you know what I find out when I get back."

"If you get back. . . . Listen, Mac. This whole deal doesn't look like it's going to end well for you. I wish I could be more supportive. I don't like disappointing you, but I have to drop out of this one. Conscience, you know." Then with a smile, Presler added, "You know what that is? Right, my brother?"

"I've talked about conscience before with a CIA operative. He didn't seem to have one. Now, I'm having my doubts as to whether or not it's a good thing to have."

"It is, believe me," said Presler. "I have one request, though."

"What's that?"

"Just try not to leave a bloody trail of bodies on your way to Brisco. That's very bad Karma."

"Can't promise you that," Mac said.

Presler shook his head. "I'm sure there's already an undercover investigation going on at those places, like all those clubs. Let the Feds handle the strip-club mutts. It's their ballgame. You and I are just a pair of retired cops. Just a blip in this world of good guys and bad guys. Remember, you are not the guardian of civilized society. If you decide to kill everyone there who doesn't cooperate with you, you'll be the one to pay the price. Unintended consequences can be killers, too."

"I see what you're saying, Marty. We just have to disagree on this one. We're looking at this from different sides. For you, the end doesn't always justify the means. For me, it always does. These dirtbags need to be taken down by any means necessary. I'm sorry you're not on board with this one." Mac then rubbed the back of his neck before adding, "I'd like to continue this discussion with you and possibly change your mind but what I really need is a few hours shuteye. I'd appreciate it if you would be so kind as to let me use your couch. Later this evening, I'll be heading to Miami. If I don't see Brisco near that Little Havana club in twenty-four hours, I'll be in Orlando. Give me a shout-out if that dirtbag is seen anywhere in your neighborhood."

2:35 PM
Miami, Florida

Brisco knocked on the rear door of the strip club. Jake, wearing a black sportscoat to hide his 9mm Smith and Wesson handgun, let him in.

"I'm here to see your boss,"

"You're a hot commodity right now, Brisco. I'm not sure he wants to see you."

"Just tell him I'm here!"

Jake left the room. Moments later Valverde entered.

"Hey, Valverde, remember me? Your ol' buddy."

"Some buddy you are. I hear everybody's looking for you."

"Yeah, well it's a bit safer down here for me right now. I had to dump your buddy's car up north. Have him report it stolen. He'll get the car back. I had to grab another guy's wheels. This one has to be dumped, too. Thankfully, there's a little less to worry about down here."

"I wouldn't be so sure."

"What da ya mean?"

"The cops had been watching Ripper's house. He couldn't get me the three grand you owed me, personally, so he sent someone, who I don't know, drop off the money."

"Who was that?"

"Some guy named Manny Hernández."

"Who?"

"Manny Hernández."

"I never heard of him, either. Ripper never mentioned a guy by that name. And I would have known him if he was dealing in any way with our boy. Something ain't right here, Benito."

"If you don't know this guy, then we've got a problem."

"We?"

"The money was for the car you were driving. If Snake was compromised in any way, whoever put the squeeze on him knows what that three grand was for."

"Then meet with this guy again and see who he is and what he knows."

"I'll do that. What about Snake? Were you able to get in touch with him?"

"I'm not calling him. If the cops are watching his house, they're probably also tapping his phone. I'd hate to think he was arrested for something and is working with them. This guy Manny could very well be a cop."

"If that's the case, maybe it's best not to meet with him again. I don't want cops knowing anything about our business."

"Just meet with him and play it cool. You know not to give him any incriminating information. If he's an undercover, he'll probably be wired up. So, make it sound like you're running a legit operation."

"Why go through all this?"

"For two reasons. One, to get him off your back. And two, to find out if Snake is a rat. In which case, he goes on the kill list."

"You can't kill everyone who crosses you."

"Wanna bet? Now tell your buddy I need another car. The one I'm driving is way too hot."

"If Snake turned, the money is gone. What are you going to pay me with, I.O.U.s?"

"Don't worry about that. I have my own stash. Do you honestly think I' would've left all my cash with Snake?" Brisco then looked directly into Valverde's eyes and said, "I don't trust anyone, including your ol' buddy."

Valverde noticed the bulge on Brisco side. "Okay, I'll see about another car. It'll be two grand, since you paid me for the five hundred I fronted you and for the gun and ammo."

"It'll be one grand, and I'll need it by tomorrow!"

Valverde realized that Brisco was now teetering on the edge of sanity—the result of pressure from the police, betrayal from friends and associates, and from the massive amount of 'roid-rage building inside him. So, Valverde decided to ease up on the ex-con. Fearing Brisco could snap at any time should anything trigger a response, Valverde took the less aggressive approach. He decided to play nice. "How will I get in touch with you?" was all he said.

"Just have the car here tomorrow. I'll stop back sometime in the afternoon. And I'll bring the cash. In the meantime, you better clean house."

After Brisco left, Valverde got his crew together and told them to reroute the illegals at the club to his place in Orlando, and to relocate any incriminating photos and documents from the club to Maggie's house just outside Miami. He also told his crew to watch their step around Brisco that he was getting near the breaking point.

5:10 PM
Miami, Florida

"I got your call, Benito. How can I help you?" said Sanchez.

"Let's go in the back, Manny," replied Valverde, "where it's more private."

He then led Sanchez to an office in the rear of the strip club.

"Have a seat," he said as he pushed a chair by the corner of his desk. Valverde then hit an intercom button. "Come join us," he said.

In a moment Maggie entered the room with a well-dressed man who sat in a chair by the door.

"This is Luther, my accountant. You know Maggie our bookkeeper," said Valverde. "Luther handles my financial transactions and taxes. I want him to hear who you are and what you do. Okay?"

"Yeah, sure," said Sanchez. "What do you need from me?"

"Some answers."

"Like what?"

"Like who the hell are you? I did a little homework on you and your business," replied Valverde.

"Oh, really. What'd ya find out?"

"Not a whole hell of a lot. Nothing on you or the company you work for. Now, that's strange, isn't it, Manny?"

"No. We run a very private business."

"No business dealing in the amounts of money you profess to deal in is *that* private. And, you. Nothing on the 'Net. Oh, yeah. People with your name. But not you. Now, that's strange, isn't it, Manny? Even my girls have footprints online."

"What can I tell you? I keep a low profile."

"Not really. I thought I saw you before. You were at my club one time before. And there were new faces at the bar the last time you and your partner were here. There's a guy in the bar right now who's new. Most guys who come here are repeat customers from the neighborhood. My girls know many of them personally, if you know what I mean. They don't know who those guys were, or this new guy today, and neither do any of my customers. What about that, Manny? If that's your name."

"What the hell are you talking about? I did Snake a favor dropping off the money for you. I don't need this shit. *You* asked me about my business. *I* didn't ask you."

Just then there was a knock on the office door.

Valverde nodded to Luther, who got up and opened it. In walked the new customer escorted by Jake.

"Do you know this guy, Manny?"

Sanchez looked his cover in the eyes and said, "Never seen him before."

"Well, here's the deal. I suspect you work for some police department, state or federal agency. We're not involved in any illegal activity. We run a respectable business here. I don't know what the story is with you and Rameriz, but it'd be best if we never see each other again. That includes your buddy here and the two guys who were at the bar the last time you were here."

"Too bad it didn't work out between us," said Sanchez.

Ryan Cabrero and Miami Vice cop Adam Rose listened to the receiver as they sat in the unmarked car down the block from the strip club.

"Looks like this case just went completely belly-up," said Cabrero after hearing the takedown words 'didn't work out.' He then signaled the other undercover officers in the area to enter the club.

Within 30 seconds, eight undercovers stormed in through the front door. Two other officers took their preassigned cue to cover the rear door.

"Okay, here's what's going to happen next," said Sanchez as Cabrero and two other undercovers forced their way into the room.

"This here is my partner, Agent Cabrero. We and the other agents by the bar are going to interview all your dancers, barmaids, and bouncers before we leave here. We find any criminal activity or civil irregularities, we will close you down. Best for you to contact your attorney."

"Where's your warrant?" asked Valverde.

"Don't need one to interview your employees. But we do happen to have a subpoena for you to produce your employee and financial records." Turning to Cabrero, Sanchez said, "Ryan, please do the honors."

Cabrero held the subpoena in his hand. He walked toward Valverde who was now on his feet. Cabrero pressed the warrant to Valverde's chest. "Here, give this to your lawyer when he arrives."

20
AUGUST 23, 2015

8:30 AM
BAYONNE, NEW JERSEY

Local police were notified that a floater was discovered down by the drydock. The body was fished out and sent to the Essex County Medical Examiner's Office in Newark for identification and autopsy. The postmortem exam, which included fingerprints, dental records, and missing-person reports, revealed that the victim, James Andersen, age 75, was reported missing from his East Orange home by his daughter on August 20. Her dad was reported to be going out to buy food items. A check with the food mart revealed that he never made it there. He was expected home on the afternoon of the 20, but hadn't been seen since the morning of that day by any family member. The mode of death was listed as a C2 cervical fracture, the result of strangulation; the cause of Mr. Andersen's demise, therefore, was ruled a homicide.

Despite an exhaustive investigation, Mr. Andersen's car was not found, nor the wallet his family members said he always had on him. An attempt to locate the 2008 light-blue Honda Accord, with its NJ license plate number, was put out over the police airwaves.

2:53 PM
Orlando, Florida

"I didn't want to call you, but I might need a favor," Valverde said. "I'm in Orlando. The cops are all over me right now. I had a lot of the girls shipped up here yesterday after talking with you. Good thing we had that conversation, Bull. Your boy is not a snake. He's a rat. His buddy Manny is a cop. Those bastards tried to scam me. When I called their bluff, they dropped a subpoena on me yesterday for my employee and financial records."

"Were any of the trafficked girls questioned?"

"Fortunately, not. I had them sent here to Chicas after talking with you yesterday and before they dropped the subpoena on me. I'll move them out of here later this evening. These bastards are probably getting ready to drop a search warrant on my businesses. So, I have to clean them all out—putas, drugs, guns, cash.

"In the meantime, I have a car for you around back. I have a guy who'll dispose of the car you're driving now. Just leave the keys in it.

"They interviewed a handful of employees last night. All the legit ones, and they listed a Grand Jury date for me to produce business records. Maggie was able to get up here last night. I suspect they'll eventually want to interview all the girls here, too, but I plan on moving all the illegals out of the club, the massage parlor, and the escort office by tonight. I have a private group that will pay for the girls and disperse them across the state to other buyers. I'm going to need your help on doing that. You okay with that? If so, forget the car bill."

"Sure, why not? I've got every cop on the East Coast looking for me. I might as well transport a carload of trafficked females for the fun of it," Brisco said. "Just call me if you see any cop activity in the area."

5:00 PM
Orlando, Florida

Mac sat in his truck a block down from Chicas, Chicas, Chicas. He had a clear view of the front door and entrance to its adjacent alleyway. He wolfed down a cheese sandwich and soda that Marty had given him before he left Sarasota. It was then he got a good look at the driver of a light-blue Accord who passed slowly by him and pulled into the alley. *Brisco!*

Mac checked his .45 holstered on his left hip and his .40 cal tucked in the small of his back. He then reached under the front passenger seat and removed a black tire iron. He got out of his truck and walked to the front door of Chicas. Once inside, one of Valverde's men saw Mac approach with the tire iron in his left hand.

"Hey, you!" shouted the muscle as he reached for his gun on his right hip, under his shirt.

Mac quickly swung the iron, striking the man on his right wrist, breaking it. He then swung the iron onto the left knee of the bouncer, dropping him to the floor. The man yelled out as Mac then killed him with one swift swing of the tire iron to the head.

As this was happening, the dancers, waitresses, barmaids, and handful of customers pushed their way past Mac and the bouncer, heading for the front door.

"What the hell is going on!" yelled Jake coming out from the backroom after hearing all the commotion. When he saw Mac standing over his partner, tire iron in hand, he reached for his gun. Mac dropped the iron, drew his .45, and placed two bullets into Jake—one in the head and one in the chest.

He then picked up the tire iron, stepped over Jake's body and walked into the back room where Valverde, Maggie, and Brisco stood. Brisco was behind the desk, just to the left of the two. Both Brisco and Valverde were armed. Brisco got off the first round hitting

Mac in the right shoulder. Mac threw the iron at Brisco, striking him in the chest. The force of the blow and the weakened grip on the weapon as a result of the prior injury caused Brisco to drop the gun. It slid under the desk to where Mac was standing. Valverde ran farther to the left of Brisco and got off a rushed shot, hitting Mac in the left thigh. Mac fired three rounds at Valverde—one each to the stomach, chest, and head. He died instantly. Maggie, unarmed, screamed and ran from the room.

Before Mac could turn back, Brisco had picked up the metal office chair and threw it at him, hitting him in the injured leg and left arm, causing Mac to drop his .45.

"Just you and me," said Brisco as he bent over and reached under the desk for his gun on the floor. Realizing it was too far out of reach, he turned over the metal desk and slid it toward the man he longed to kill. Mac grabbed his backup weapon. Taking the .40 cal from the small of his back, he began to raise it toward Brisco. Mac fired several rushed rounds, hitting the desk twice and Brisco twice—once in the upper chest area and once in the shoulder. Brisco, fighting for his life, jumped over the desk and barreled into Mac before he could get off another round. Both men fell to the floor.

Brisco still had the strength of a lion with all the drug enhancements he'd been taking. He grabbed Mac's left wrist and pounded it into the floor. Mac dropped his gun, letting it fall several feet away. Before Brisco could reach out and pick it up, Mac ground his right thumb into Brisco's left eye. With Brisco leaning over attempting to reach the gun, Mac was able to knee him in the groin, then flip him off with a swift kick from his right leg.

Brisco crawled toward the gun. He reached it, but as he turned on his knees to shoot, he was struck a glancing blow across the face with the tire iron. He sustained two more glancing blows before he was able to get several rushed shots off, most of which ended up in the wall behind Mac. One bullet, however, hit him in the stomach.

With Brisco now on his back, Mac grabbed his wrist and tried wrestling the gun from his hand. Brisco fired one more round, missing Mac's head by inches. The gun-slide locked back after the last shot, indicating the gun was empty of rounds. Mac summoned up enough adrenalin to try and hit Brisco one more time with the tire iron. Brisco recovered slightly and with overpowering strength, from years of steroid use and power training, blocked the strike at his head and threw Mac off him.

Dazed and bleeding, Brisco staggered to his feet and picked up the metal chair. Mac quickly noticed Brisco's gun—which had slid in front of the overturned desk and now laid in front of it— within arm's reach. He picked it up and went to fire it, but Brisco was quicker. He swung the chair down on Mac's hand that held the gun. He then quickly put his foot on Mac's wrist. As Mac lay on the floor, all his energy fading, Brisco pried the gun from his hand.

Aiming the gun at Mac's head, Brisco said, "Finally. I win, dirt-bag cop!"

As he was about to pull the trigger, six .357 rounds burst into his chest. The blasts, like a sledgehammer, sent Brisco reeling backwards. He was dead before he hit the floor. Brisco's eyes remained open and his mouth agape.

Marty Presler stood over him. "No, *you* lose, asshole!"

Mac looked up and, with foggy eyes, saw Presler.

He smiled. "Marty, Marty . . . why are you . . . here?"

Marty quickly got on his knees next to Mac and tore open his shirt. Looking down at the bullet wound to Mac's stomach, he knew the outcome was not going to be good. There was little bleeding outside the wound, but Marty knew how catastrophic the internal damage would be as that hot lead bullet would tear up organs and vital blood vessels. "I've been shadowing you since yesterday. You know I couldn't desert you, brother," he said.

"Is Brisco dead?" Mac asked between clenched teeth.

"He'd better be. I unloaded my .357 into him."

"Thanks, Marty."

"I owed you that one, partner."

Mac was starting to fade, but was able to ask, "Why'd you come? You didn't want to."

"I couldn't let my best friend and patrol partner go into the lion's den alone. I wish I had gotten here earlier, though. You might have been in better shape."

"It's over, partner."

"No, Mac. It's not! Stay focused. You're going to make it. When I pulled up, I heard the shots. I called for backup and an ambulance. I knew when I heard all the noise and people running out of the club that someone *wasn't* going to make it. I was hoping it wasn't going to be you 'cause I know how you can get."

Mac forced a smile.

"Just hang in there a bit longer. You can do it, Mac. I know you can."

Mac struggled to get the next words out. "Too late. . . . Please . . . tell . . . Cheryl . . . and . . . Hope . . . I love . . . them."

"Hang tough, Mac. You're gonna make it! I know you."

"Please . . . tell . . . the . . . girls . . . I'm . . . sorry."

"Don't be sorry. Nothing to be sorry about. I'm with you, brother. Don't give up! Don't give up!"

"Cheryl . . . knows . . . I'm . . . the . . . scorpion. I couldn't change I . . . wanted . . . to. I … couldn't. But … I … love … them."

Mac then closed his eyes. Marty heard the rattle, the last gasp for breath. He knew his brother in blue was gone.

8:30 PM
Bloomfield, New Jersey

Cheryl heard the knock on the door. *Who could that be at this hour?* she thought.

Opening the door, she saw the Newark Chief of Police, the Bloomfield Chief of Police, and two Patrol Officers. Behind them were Jason, Ann, and Father Nick Polsani.

"What's going on?! Why. . . oh, no . . . no. no, no! Where's Mac? Where's my husband?!"

The Newark chief was the first to speak. "I'm so sorry to have to tell you. Your husband is dead. He died a hero."

"No! I don't want to hear this! He's not dead!" As Cheryl then fell back, up against the wall, Ann pushed her way through and hugged her. Jason grabbed her hand and said, "Mac saved a lot of people down there, sis. That's what Mac's friend Marty Presler said. He didn't want to call you directly. Not something he wanted to do over the phone. So he called the two police departments and me. He said he'd call you later to pay his respects and to let you know the details of what happened."

"I don't want to talk with him right now, Jason! Mac wouldn't have gone down there following that nut job if he wasn't looking for Marty. I told Mac to let the police handle it. But he couldn't do that for us. I want my husband! I love him, and I let him go. I told him I didn't want him to go. He went anyway.

"Oh, my God. What am I going to tell Hope? How do I tell her that her dad is gone?"

"We'll do that," said Ann, "if you want us to. It would make it easier."

"No, no. Oh, my God. How can I do this? My poor baby. Father, will you come upstairs with me to tell Hope?"

"Of course, Cheryl."

Father Polsani and Cheryl mounted the stairs as Ann directed her husband and the police officers into the kitchen. The somber group sat quietly waiting Cheryl's return to discuss funeral arrangements. As they waited, the silence was suddenly broken by the muffled cries of a young girl coming from upstairs.

21

AUGUST 28, 2015

4:30 PM
NEWARK, NEW JERSEY

Marty arrived in Newark International Airport with Mac's body in the cargo bay. A police escort awaited. In the company of Mac's wife, daughter, brother- and sister-in-law and their children, the escort transported his body to the funeral parlor in Bloomfield.

Two days later, many local citizens and law enforcement personnel visited the parlor to pay their respects. One rather pretty, middle-aged woman, draped in black, approached the casket and touched the folded hands of Mac's body. She looked familiar to Cheryl, but she didn't or couldn't say why she knew her. The woman then turned and left the parlor.

Cheryl got up and walked over to Presler. "Marty, who was that woman who was just at the casket?"

"That was Mac's first wife, Janet."

"Yes! That's where I've seen her before. I've seen old photos of her; and Mac pointed her out once when we were in the food store and she walked in. He smiled and said, 'Hi.' She just walked by as if we didn't exist."

"Yeah, she's a tough one. She never forgave Mac for their pregnant daughter's death. I'm surprised she came. She wouldn't acknowledge me or any other cop in the department after that happened. I guess with Mac's death, in a weird sort of way, she has closure. Maybe now she can let some of the pain and hard feelings go."

"You think she's forgiven him now? Not that he needed any forgiveness."

"I wouldn't go that far."

"It wasn't his fault his daughter got mixed up with the wrong people. He did try getting her out of that sick group."

"Well, no convincing Janet of that. That's been the baggage she's been carrying all these years . . . and I guess she'll be carrying it till the day she dies." He then added, "Still, I'm amazed she showed up . . . and all in black. Go figure."

22
AUGUST 31, 2015

9:50 AM
NEWARK, NEW JERSEY

Several hundred uniformed police officers lined up on Broadway across from St. Michael's Church awaiting the arrival of the hearse carrying Mac's body. Father Polsani was in the sacristy preparing to place a white robe over his black priestly garb when Cheryl entered.

"Father, may I speak with you?"

"Of course, Cheryl."

"May I make confession?"

He directed her to chairs in the corner. "Let's sit down."

"Father, can God forgive me for telling Mac that Hope and I wouldn't be there for him if he left?" Cheryl began to cry.

"Oh, Cheryl. Please don't cry. Marty told me Mac's last words were that he loved you two. And I know you loved him very much. I could see it in the way you cared about him. And he needed that. He needed someone like you in his life. What should God forgive you for? One must sin in order to ask for forgiveness. You were simply concerned for your husband's well-being, for his safety in a dangerous world. That was your job as a loving wife. God knows your heart, and your heart was pure in that moment. You were just trying to protect him in your own way. But if forgiveness is what you are looking for from God, He forgives you. He forgives you for the underserved burden you placed on your soul. Mac had already forgiven you by professing his love for you at the moment he was going to meet God.

"Now, there is only one person left who needs to forgive you . . . and that person is *you*. You need to forgive yourself. Don't carry that undeserved burden. It will darken your life. Only let those good times you two shared together take up space in your head, heart, and soul. Will you do that, Cheryl?"

Wiping tears from her eyes, she said, "Thank you, Father. I'll try. I will. I promise."

When it was time for Father Polsani to address the congregation, he stood behind the pulpit, looked out among the throng of churchgoers and, remembering his prior talk in the hospital chapel when Mac was fighting for his life, said, "I feel I've done this before." Those who were there at the hospital nodded in agreement.

Father Polsani then looked down at the opened Bible before him, and read the words from Psalm 58:

> "The righteous will rejoice when they
>   see vengeance done;
> they will bathe their feet in the
>   blood of the wicked.
> People will say, 'Surely there is
>   reward for the righteous;
> Surely there is a God who judges on
>   earth.

"So wrote David while in exile. The same man who slayed Goliath. The one who God said was a man after His own heart. David was old school. An Old Testament God-fearing man. An eye for an eye, tooth for a tooth kind of guy. Let's face it. That's the kind of guy Mac was.

"Mac was cut from a warrior's cloth. He took on the mantel of God's soldier for good in this world. Fighting evil was in his blood. He was a soldier for good, to a point, however, where—let's be honest, after all we are in a church—Mac saw justice where others saw vengeance. He sometimes had his role a bit confused. I think Mac, at times, believed he was the last bastion against evil. I tried to convince him otherwise . . . on many occasions. It was not his job alone to save the world. Our Lord Jesus took on that burden. Still, we all have a part to play in this just battle against evil. Nonetheless, Mac walked that tightrope between justice and vengeance. As Scripture tells us in Romans 12:

> " Avenge not yourselves. . . . Vengeance belongs
> unto me, saith the Lord. It is mine to repay.
> I will avenge. Do not let evil defeat you, but
> defeat evil by doing good."

Peering down from the pulpit to Cheryl, Hope, Jason, Ann, and their children in the front pew, Father Polsani said, "And Mac did good in his life. He was a caring, loving husband, father, friend, and," looking at Marty and the other former and active police officers filling the pews and along the aisles throughout the church, "he was a loyal brother officer. A man who wanted desperately to serve and protect, however he could. His inspiration must have been St. Michael, the patron saint of our church here. Coincidentally, St. Michael is the patron saint of police officers, though I don't think Mac realized that during his life here with us. Back eleven years ago in that hospital chapel, when he was fighting for his life, we prayed that he would not join that army of saints. Not yet. That we would have him for many more years. That prayer was answered. But now was the time of his calling. I suspect his next assignment will be working with St. Michael." A low laughter filled the church.

"I've known Mac Taylor even before he was called Mac Taylor. When he was a kid in his twenties, a descendant of Scottish Highlanders. A kid known as Donald MacPherson who ran through the jungles of a place on the other side of the world called Vietnam. That was a while back, where some of you have already heard that that young man saved my life and the lives of many other soldiers. Then, as a police officer, he continued spending years of service helping others. Even after retiring from the police force, Mac took on the role of private investigator where his exploits helping people and protecting the security of our country continued. And even until death, we see Mac giving his life fighting evil to protect innocent lives.

Let us remember Mac as the good man he was. A man who battled evil in the only way he knew how, with every fiber of his being for the people he loved. And that's the point of Mac Taylor's life. There are many out there, way too many, who fight on the side of evil. They fight out of hatred, out of pride, for power or wealth, for control over the lives of others. That was not our good friend Mac Taylor. He fought out of love—love for his family, for his friends, and for his country. The lesson to be learned today from Mac Taylor's sacrifice is that we each have to find our own pathway to fighting evil. Mac found his. We all must find our own. It is our purpose to stand on the side of goodness, honor, justice, and, mostly, love; and to defend those virtues. All of us. We must lead that purposeful life. That life of meaning. A life loving God, loving each other, and a life fighting the good fight as Mac had done *his* whole life. Otherwise, our stay here is meaning*less*. If we're not confronting and defeating evil—either by justifiable force or peaceful resistance—every time we encounter it, well, then, I suspect, instead, we're all just here . . . just here . . . killing time. So, strive to live that purposeful, meaningful life. Live that life of love, justice, and sacrifice After all, those *were* the virtues our brother, Mac Taylor, lived for and died for."

Father Polsani then looked down on Mac's coffin by the altar rail and finished his homily with these words, "Rest well, my friend, my brother. You served *your* time here with honor. May you now find eternal peace and comfort in the arms of our Lord and Savior, Jesus Christ. Amen."

23
SEPTEMBER 8, 2015

8:20 AM
ORLANDO/MIAMI, FLORIDA

Immediately following the shootout at Chicas, Chicas, Chicas, the Department for Homeland Security's Center for Countering Human Trafficking executed search warrants on the Orlando club along with Valverde's escort service and massage parlor in that city, and his club, massage parlor and escort service in Miami. Warrants were also executed at Valverde's house where $1.2 million in cash and a large amount of drugs were found. In addition, due to the incriminating evidence provided by the confidential informant on Valverde's drug organization, the U.S. Drug Enforcement Agency opened its own investigation into Valverde's chain of operations.

Moreover, during the execution of the warrants, twelve individuals connected with Valverde's criminal enterprise were arrested for crimes ranging from kidnapping and assault to drug and sex trafficking. In a deal with the prosecutor, one of the individuals arrested, Maglia "Maggie" Selina, gave a statement regarding the criminal enterprise. A search of her home in Miami revealed photos, documents and identifications taken from the women who were sex-trafficked at the clubs, escort services and massage parlors. Fraudulent documents drafted as cover for the sex-trafficked females were recovered, also.

The Enforcement and Removal Operations section of DHS was able to remove eleven missing young girls of the thirty-one total number of females who were being trafficked by Valverde and his cohorts. After things settled down a bit, several prominent Cuban Americans in the Miami area, in conjunction with the Florida Coalition Against Human Trafficking (FCAHT), asked to help the young women. One woman in particular, Maria Consuelo Alvarez Rodriguez, was sponsored and funded by the private group to open her own boutique just west of downtown Miami in the Cuban community known as Little Havana. Her first employees were two other trafficked females. With the approval of Florida's Department of Children and Family, Jill Morgan and Maureen Sorbo left their sorrowful past few months behind and prepared to learn the skills of dressmaking from their dear friend, Maria. Well-wishers from Little Havana came out to celebrate and support the opening of Maria's new dress boutique which she named El Sueño de la Rosa— Rosa's Dream—in dedication to her beloved aunt.

8:34 AM
Casperson Beach, Florida

Marty opened his beach chair and sat down. He pulled his cap over his eyes and listened as the Gulf waves landed ever so softly, repeatedly, endlessly on the Caspersen shore. An early morning rain provided a double rainbow of brilliant colors. It was then he remembered the last time he sat here and was thankful he survived the moment. If it hadn't been for his daughter and her family arriving at the exact time his intended killer had, he would not be here and the history of what followed would have been so much different. Then, thinking about the last few weeks, he was more thankful than ever before that he lived to share those last fleeting moments of his best friend's life. Marty knew, though, that the end was nearer for Mac than he wanted to believe. In his mind, he knew Mac's style of loyalty, honor, and action was a throwback to another time. Not a cop for today's standard, but perfectly suited to be an old guard; like those courageous men of centuries past, who with only a sword, axe, and shield fought with reckless abandonment alongside other courageous men; men like fellow Scotsman Robert the Bruce. Had Mac been at the Battle of Bannockburn, fighting against the English for Scotland's independence, Marty had no doubt Mac would have led the charge that changed Scottish history. That's just how Marty pictured him: brave and committed; somewhat anachronistic, somewhat iconoclastic; the image at times of the lone warrior, a loyal clansman. But more particularly, he saw his trusted, street partner, as a brother-in-arms, united by combat, always fighting on the side of right for the people he loved in the temporal battles of life.

After a few minutes, with his feet dug into the warm sand, Martin Presler began to drift off. It was then he was drawn back thirty-some years to that June morning in Newark when he and Mac responded to the call that started the whole chain of events. Those radio transmissions would echo in his mind for many more years:

"Two to HQ, we're on Sixth now and we have an eyeball on the suspect. Five could you respond to the scene? We'll grab this guy."

"Five received."

8:53 AM
BLOOMFIELD, NEW JERSEY

Early September in New Jersey brings new beginnings: new problems, new focuses, new hopes, new life. Back to work; back to school; back to paying attention to politics, the stock market, a time to shop for fall clothes, and to offer greater commitment to yardwork. The days soon get cooler, then colder, then much shorter; leaves coat the ground and gutters; and athletes get more serious as the fall sports season moves along. That's how it was last fall in Bloomfield, New Jersey; how it was every year before, and how it will be every year after in Bloomfield.

Cheryl knew that in her heart, but could not shake the emptiness she felt for the loss of her husband. She now saw the world in black and white, with an occasional splash of color. Pondering her loss, Cheryl knew after a few more weeks, Mac would be forgotten by most of the people who attended the funeral. For those who didn't know him personally, his name was just an article in the newspaper for a day, maybe two, three, or four. After that, he'd be forgotten. People say they'll remember, but they don't. Their lives and memories go on to other things with the distance of time. Only the close ones remember. This was what Cheryl was thinking as she accompanied Hope up the concrete stairs of the elementary school.

"I'll see you later," Cheryl said as she kissed Hope on the forehead. A splash of color appeared.

"Bye, Mom. I love you."

"I love you, too," Cheryl said, before taking a deep breath and heading off to her new office as school nurse. Once inside, she reached into her pocketbook and removed the round, glass object containing the string that Mac had given her back in Mongaup Pond. Placing the globe on her desk, Cheryl said, barely above a whisper, "Life goes on here, but no matter what the world throws at me from now on, Sergeant Mac Taylor, my love, I will never forget you."

24

HOMEWARD BOUND

The Clock Stopped Ticking

Mac found himself standing in a field of gold, wheat stalks just to his knees. Two hawks were circling above in a crystal blue sky. They appeared like feathers dancing about. His long-lost parents suddenly appeared, accompanied by old friends, no longer living. His heart began to pound as they approached. Within an instant, he felt the warmth of their presence. Then, just as quickly, they parted. A young man in military attire walked forward. *Hi, Mac, or should I say, Don? Remember me? Joe Taylor.* The young soldier grinned and said, *Thank you, Sergeant.* Then, looking over his shoulder, he added, *There's someone else who wants to see you.*

In the distance, Mac could see a young woman dancing with a child. As the pair danced closer, becoming clearer, a broad smile burst across his face. His eyes welled up with tears. The dancing girl stopped within arm's length and extended a hand. *Hello, Dad. We've been waiting for you.*

The child, a little boy, poked his head out from behind her dress. *Who are you?* asked Mac.

This is your grandson, Dad, said his daughter, Rachel. *His name is Donnie.*

Mac's broad smile widened a bit more. *Hello, Donnie,* he said.

The little boy ran to him and hugged him about the waist.

Now, it's time for us to bring you home, Dad, said Rachel.

Mac kissed his daughter and grandson. Then, hand-in-hand, the three caught up with his parents and company of friends from his past, and all of them headed toward the bright light just ahead.